Arthur C. Auchmuty

Poems of English Heroism from Brunanburh to Lucknow,

from Athelstan to Albert. Collected and arranged, with notes historical and

illustrative.

Arthur C. Auchmuty

Poems of English Heroism from Brunanburh to Lucknow,
from Athelstan to Albert. Collected and arranged, with notes historical and illustrative.

ISBN/EAN: 9783337214241

Printed in Europe, USA, Canada, Australia, Japan

Cover: Foto ©Andreas Hilbeck / pixelio.de

More available books at **www.hansebooks.com**

POEMS OF

ENGLISH HEROISM

POEMS OF
ENGLISH HEROISM

FROM BRUNANBURH TO LUCKNOW

FROM ATHELSTAN TO ALBERT

COLLECTED AND ARRANGED

WITH NOTES HISTORICAL AND ILLUSTRATIVE

BY

ARTHUR COMPTON AUCHMUTY, M.A.

"Love thou thy land, with love far-brought
From out the storied Past"

NEW EDITION

LONDON

KEGAN PAUL, TRENCH, TRÜBNER & CO., Ltᴰ

PATERNOSTER HOUSE, CHARING CROSS ROAD

1895

TO

KENNETH-CHARLES

COMPTON-HENRY

AND

JANET-FRANCES

WITH ALL OTHER ENGLISH BOYS AND GIRLS

"HEIRS OF ALL THE AGES"

A POSY OF FLOWERS

FROM THE FIELD OF THEIR

NATIONAL HERITAGE

CONTENTS.

—◦◦◦—

POEMS OF ENGLISH HEROISM.

I.

BATTLE OF BRUNANBURH.

I.

ATHELSTAN King,
Lord among Earls,
Bracelet-bestower and
Baron of Barons,
He with his brother,
Edmund Atheling,
Gaining a lifelong
Glory in battle,
Slew with the sword-edge
There by Brunanburh,
Brake the shield-wall,
Hew'd the lindenwood,
Hack'd the battleshield,
Sons of Edward with hammer'd brands.

B

II.

Theirs was a greatness
Got from their Grandsires—
Theirs that so often in
Strife with their enemies
Struck for their hoards and their hearths and their
homes.

III.

Bow'd the spoiler,
Bent the Scotsman,
Fell the shipcrews
Doom'd to the death.
All the field with blood of the fighters
Flow'd, from when first the great
Sun-star of morningtide,
Lamp of the Lord God
Lord everlasting,
Glode over earth till the glorious creature
Sunk to his setting.

IV.

There lay many a man
Marr'd by the javelin,
Men of the Northland
Shot over shield.
There was the Scotsman
Weary of war.

V.

We the West-Saxons,
Long as the daylight
Lasted, in companies
Troubled the track of the host that we hated,
Grimly with swords that were sharp from the grindstone,
Fiercely we hack'd at the flyers before us.

VI.

Mighty the Mercian,
Hard was his hand-play.
Sparing not any of
Those that with Anlaf,
Warriors over the
Weltering waters
Borne in the bark's-bosom,
Drew to this island,
Doom'd to the death.

VII.

Five young kings put asleep by the sword-stroke,
Seven strong Earls of the army of Anlaf
Fell on the war-field, numberless numbers,
Shipmen and Scotsmen.

VIII.

Then the Norse leader,
·   Dire was his need of it,

Few were his following,
Fled to his warship :
Fleeted his vessel to sea with the king in it,
Saving his life on the fallow flood.

IX.

Also the crafty one,
Constantínus,
Crept to his North again,
Hoar-headed hero !

X.

Slender reason had
He to be proud of
The welcome of war-knives—
He that was reft of his
Folk and his friends that had
Fallen in conflict,
Leaving his son too
Lost in the carnage,
Mangled to morsels,
A youngster in war !

XI.

Slender reason had
He to be glad of
The clash of the war-glaive—
Traitor and trickster
And spurner of treaties —

He nor had Anlaf
With armies so broken
A reason for bragging
That they had the better
In perils of battle
On places of slaughter—
The struggle of standards,
The rush of the javelins,
The crash of the charges,
The wielding of weapons—
The play that they play'd with
The children of Edward.

XII.

Then with their nail'd prows
Parted the Norsemen, a
Blood-redden'd relic of
Javelins over
The jarring breaker, the deepsea billow
Shaping their way toward Dyflen again,
Shamed in their souls.

XIII.

Also the brethren,
King and Atheling,
Each in his glory,
Went to his own in his own West-Saxonland,
Glad of the war.

XIV.

Many a carcase they left to be carrion,
Many a livid one, many a sallow-skin—
Left for the white-tail'd eagle to tear it, and
Left for the horny-nibb'd raven to rend it, and
Gave to the garbaging war-hawk to gorge it, and
That gray beast, the wolf of the weald.

XV.

Never had huger
Slaughter of heroes
Slain by the sword-edge—
Such as old writers
Have writ of in histories—
Hapt in this isle, since
Up from the East hither
Saxon and Angle from
Over the broad billow
Broke into Britain with
Haughty war-workers who
Harried the Welshman, when
Earls that were lured by the
Hunger of glory gat
Hold of the land.

TENNYSON (*from the Old English*).

II.

THE FIGHT OF MALDON.

I.

*　　*　　*　　*　　○

THEN 'gan Brihtnoth
His men to array :
Rode past and rank'd them,
Taught them their places,
Bade them their round shields
Hold fast with hand-grip,
At nothing frighten'd.
When he his folk thus
Had duly order'd,
There down he lighted
'Mid whom he wist
Dearest and faithfullest,
Bands of his hearth.

II.

Then stood forth stern-voiced on the river-brink
Wiking's herald, and thrill'd out a threatening
Sea-folk's errand across to the Earl.

III.

" Me have they hither sent,
They, the swift sea-farers,

Bade me say thus to thee :
'Send, for thy safety's sake,
Bracelets right speedily ;
Better the spear-rush ye
Buy off with gift-money
Than in hard-foughten fight
Slaying where no need is
Either the other.
List ye this thing to do,
Fast shall a peace be made,
Clench'd with the gold.'
Haply thou holdest thee,
Thou that here richest art,
Willing to free thy folk,
Paying the seamen's price,
Peace to win peaceably,—
So with the scot will we
Back to our ships, and sail
Forth on our fleet, and hold
Peace with you still."

IV.

Out spake Brihtnoth,
His shield upheaving,
Shook the slight ash-shaft, and
Fierce and unflinching
With words made answer.

V.

" Hearest thou, sea-farer,
What this folk saith to thee?
This is the gift ye shall
Take of them,—javelins,
Spear-point and sword-edge,
Heriot of weapons, but
Not for your welfare.
Turn again, therefore, thou,
Sea-people's errand-man,
Bear these ill tidings back :
Here stands a stout-hearted
Earl with his following ;
Stand for our own land we,
Home of mine Elderman,
Folk of our Athelred,
Athelred's ground !
Now shall the heathen men
Fall on the war-field.
This were, methinketh,
Shame overpassing,
Ye should on ship-board
Scot from us carry
Unbefoughten.
Fared have ye thus far
Over this earth of ours ;
But not so lightly now
Fare shall ye forth and bear

Treasure in triumph.
Judge first between us shall
Spear-point and sword-edge,
Yea, the grim battle-game,
Ere we pay tribute."

VI.

Then the Earl bade
His folk set forward,
Bearing their shield-boards,
Till by the stream-brink,
Craving to come at their
Foemen across the flood,
Every man stood :
East-Saxons' front rank
Facing the fleet-men :
There over Panta's stream
The wikings waited
Eager for warfare.

VII.

Then he, the chieftain and helper of heroes,
Bade hold the bridge a stout war-worker, Wulfstan :
Ceola's son was he :
He with his javelin
Shot down the foremost man,
Him that there boldest set
Foot on the bridge.
There stood with Wulfstan

Warmen unfearing,
Alfere and Maccus,
High-mettled twain.
Theirs not to flinch nor flee :
Fast at the ford they stood,
Beating the foemen back,
Till they no longer might
Brandish their weapons.

VIII.

Bitter the work that the bridge-warders wrought for
    them :
Sorely it irk'd them, the strangers, the hated ones :
Crafty they craved to cross over and close with them.
Yielded the headstrong Earl in his hardihood,
    Brihthelm's bairn, o'er the water calling :
    Hearken'd the warmen.

IX.

"Lo ! we give ground to you :
Come o'er and fight with us.
God wotteth which shall stand
Last in the slaughter-place."

X.

Waded the slaughter-wolves ;
Reck'd not for water they :
Host of the wikings.
West over Panta's stream

Bearing their linden shields
Came they to land.

XI.

Then men closed in the glory of battle-strokes :
Then was the hour for the falling of fated ones :
Shouts from the earth arose :
Ravens wheel'd round above,
Eagles for feasting fain,
Greedy for corpses.
Fast from their hands flew the
File-harden'd spears, and the
Stone-whetted javelins :
Bows were busy, and shields were dinted,
Bitter the battle-rush,
Warriors fell :
Youths lay dead on the earth around.

XII.

Then drew nigh in his fierceness the fell one,
Fenced with his shield and his weapons upheaving,
Facing the hero.
Drew to the meeting
Earl against Churl :
Either for other
Evil was thinking.
There flew a dart then
Shot from the seamen's side ;
Therewith was wounded

The lord of warriors.
Then with shield thrusting
Knapp'd he the spear-shaft—
Wroth was the hero :
He with his javelin
Pierced the proud wiking,
Wounding his wounder.
Blithe was the Earl, and he laugh d in his lustihood ;
Own'd the good day's work his Maker had given him ;
Praised and gave thanks to the Lord who had prosper'd
　　him.

XIII.

Hurl'd then some fellow a
Dart from·his hands at him :
Forth it flew piercing him,
Pierced thro' the noble one,
Athelred's Thane.
Hard by his side stood
A stripling, a boy-knight,—
Deftly he drew out
The dart with the blood on it,—
Bairn of the bridge-warder,
Wulfstan's young Wulfmaer.

XIV.

Soft one stole to the spoil of the wounded :
Lusted his heart for the filching of bracelets,
The robe, and the rings, and the jewell'd brand.

Out drew Brihtnoth
His sword from the sword-case :
Broad and brown was the blade, and he bang'd it
Full on the corselet.
Swift came a back-stroke
Struck by a fleet-man,
Quelling the Earl's arm.
Out of his hands fell the
Sword with the fallow hilt ;
Might he no longer hold
Falchion, or wield again
Weapons of warfare.

XV.

Spake he a word yet,
Hoar-headed hero,
Cheering his comrades,
Bidding his brave youths
Fight ánd go forward.
Might he not long now
Fast on his feet stand ;
Look'd he to heaven :—
" Thanks be to thee, Lord,
Wielder of nations ;
Thank Thee for all the good
I in this world have known !
Now, O my Maker mild,
Need have I most that Thou

Good to my ghost shouldst grant,
E'en that my soul may pass
Safe to the Angels' land,
Where Thou art King and Lord,
In good peace journeying.
Yea, God, that never
Hell-fiends may hurt it,
Hear now my prayer !"

XVI.

Then the heathen soldiers hew'd him ;
Hew'd the twain who stood to aid him.
There on the earth they lay
Fast by their chieftain,—
Alfnoth and Wulfmaer ;
Sold they their lives.

A. C. AUCHMUTY (*from the Old English*).

———◆◆———

III.

HAROLD AND STAMFORD-BRIDGE.

Address of Harold at a Banquet after the Battle.

EARLS, Thanes, and all our countrymen ! the day,
Our day beside the Derwent will not shine
Less than a star among the goldenest hours

Of Alfred, or of Edward his great son,
Or Athelstan, or English Ironside
Who fought with Knut, or Knut who coming Dane
Died English.   Every man about his king
Fought like a king ; the king like his own man,
No better ; one for all, and all for one,
One soul ! and therefore have we shatter'd back
The hugest wave from Norseland ever yet
Surged on us, and our battle-axes broken
The Raven's wing, and dumb'd his carrion croak
From the gray sea for ever.   Many are gone—
Drink to the dead who died for us, the living
Who fought and would have died, but happier lived,
If happier be to live ; they both have life
In the large mouth of England, till *her* voice
Die with the world.

TENNYSON, *Harold,* Act IV. Sc. 3

IV.

HAROLD AND SENLAC.

William (on the field of the dead).

Wrap them together in a purple cloak
And lay them both upon the waste sea-shore
At Hastings, there to guard the land for which

He did forswear himself—a warrior—ay,
And but that Holy Peter fought for us,
And that the false Northumbrian held aloof,
And save for that chance arrow which the Saints
Sharpen'd and sent against him—who can tell?—
Three horses had I slain beneath me : twice
I thought that all was lost. Since I knew battle,
And that was from my boyhood, never yet—
No, by the splendour of God—have I fought men
Like Harold and his brethren, and his guard
Of English. Every man about his king
Fell where he stood. They loved him : and, pray God
My Normans may but move as true with me
To the door of death. Of one self-stock at first,
Make them again one people—Norman, English ;
And English, Norman ; we should have a hand
To grasp the world with, and a foot to stamp it . . .
Flat. Praise the Saints. It is over. No more blood !
I am king of England, so they thwart me not,
And I will rule according to their laws.

TENNYSON, *Harold*, Act v. Sc. 2.

C

V.

CIVIL WAR, AND THE CRUSADES.

King Henry IV. No more the thirsty entrance of
    this soil
Shall daub her lips with her own children's blood ;
No more shall trenching war channel her fields,
Nor bruise her flowerets with the armed hoofs
Of hostile paces : those opposed eyes,
Which, like the meteors of a troubled heaven,
All of one nature, of one substance bred,
Did lately meet in the intestine shock
And furious close of civil butchery,
Shall now, in mutual well-beseeming ranks,
March all one way, and be no more opposed
Against acquaintance, kindred and allies :
The edge of war, like an ill-sheathed knife,
No more shall cut his master.   Therefore, friends,
As far as to the sepulchre of Christ—
Whose soldier now, under whose blessed cross,
We are impressed, and engaged to fight—
Forthwith a power of English shall we levy ;
Whose arms were moulded in their mothers' womb
To chase these pagans in those holy fields,
Over whose acres walk'd those blessed feet,
Which fourteen hundred years ago were nail'd
For our advantage on the bitter cross.

SHAKSPERE, 1 *Henry IV.*, Act i. Sc. 1.

VI.

SIMON DE MONTFORT AND THE BATTLE OF LEWES.

A Fragment.

Now does fair England breathe again, hoping for
    liberty ;
And may the grace of God above give her prosperity !
Liken'd to dogs the Englishmen of little price were
    made ;
Now o'er their conquer'd enemies once more they
    raise their head !

The sword was strong, and many men were slaughter'd
    in the fight ;
But truth prevail'd, and traitors were turn'd to
    shameful flight ;
For the Lord God of valour the perjured men with-
    stood,
And cast His guarding shield of truth over the pure
    and good.
By sword without and fear within the one side was
    opprest ;
The other by the favouring grace of Heaven was at
    rest.

Earl Simon's faith and faithfulness all England's
  peace secure ;
He smites the rebels, calms the realm, and drooping
  hearts makes sure.
He felt that he must fight for truth, or else must truth
  betray :
To truth he gave his right hand brave, and trod the
  rugged way.

Read, read, ye men of England, of Lewes' fight my
  lay ;
For guarded by that fight ye live securely at this day.
If victory had fall'n to those who there were sorely
  chased,
The memory of England had sorely been disgraced.

  M. CREIGHTON (*from a contemporary Latin poem*).

VII.

THE BLACK PRINCE AND CRESSY.

To King Henry V.

Go, my dread lord, to your great-grandsire's tomb,
From whom you claim : invoke his warlike spirit,
And your great-uncle's, Edward the Black Prince,
Who on the French ground play'd a tragedy,
Making defeat on the full power of France,

Whiles his most mighty father on a hill
Stood smiling to behold his lion's whelp
Forage in blood of French nobility.
O noble English, that could entertain
With half their forces the full tide of France,
And let another half stand laughing by,
All out of work and cold for action !

SHAKSPERE, *King Henry V.*, Act i. Sc. 2.

VIII.

THE BLACK PRINCE ON HIS DEATH-BED.

THEN the Prince caused his chambers to be opened
And all his followers to come in,
Who in his time had served him,
And served him with a free will :
" Sirs," said he, " pardon me,
For, by the faith I owe you,
You have served me loyally,
Though I cannot of my means
Render to each his guerdon ;
But God, by His most holy name
And saints, will render it you."
Then each wept heartily
And mourn'd right tenderly.

All who were there present,
Earl, baron, and batchelor :
Then he said in a clear voice,
" I recommend to you my son,
Who is yet but young and small,
And pray that, as you served me,
So from your heart you would serve him."
Then he call'd the King his father,
And the Duke of Lancaster his brother,
And commended to them his wife,
And his son, whom he greatly loved,
And straightway entreated them ;
And each was willing to give his aid,
Each swore upon the book,
And they promised him freely
That they would comfort his son,
And maintain him in his right ;
All the princes and barons
Swore all round to this.
And the noble Prince of fame
Gave them an hundred thousand thanks.
But till then, so God aid me,
Never was seen such bitter grief,
As was at his departure.

CHANDOS.

IX.

BALLAD OF NEVILLE'S CROSS, OR DURHAM FIELD.

THE King looked toward litle Durham,
  & that hee well beheld,
that the Earle Percy was well armed,
  With his battell axe entred the feild.

the King looket againe towards litle Durham,
  4 ancyents there see hee ;
there were to standards, 6 in a valley,
  he cold not see them with his eye.

My lord of Yorke was one of them,
  My lord of Carlile was the other ;
& my Lord ffluwilliams,
  the one came with the other.

the Bishopp of Durham commanded his men,
  & shortlye he them bade,
" that never a man shold go to the feild to fight
til he had served his god."

500 priests said masse that day
  in durham in the feild ;
& afterwards, as I hard say,
  they bare both speare and sheeld.

the Bishopp of Durham orders himself to fight
  with his battell axe in hand ;
he said, "this day now I will fight
  as long as I can stand."

"& soe will I," sayd my Lord of Carlile,
  "in this faire morning gay ;"
"& soe will I," sayd my Lord ffluwilliams,
  "for Mary, that myld may."

our English archers bent their bowes
  shortlye and anon,
they shott over the Scottish oast
  & scantlye toucht a man.

"hold downe your hands," sayd the Bishopp of
    Durham,
  "my archers good and true."
the 2ᵈ shoote that thè shott
  full sore the Scottes it rue.

the Bishopp of Durham spoke on hye
  that both partyes might heare,
"be of good cheere, my merrymen all,
  the Scotts flyen, & changen there cheere !"

but as thè saidden, soe thè didden,
  they fell on heapes hye ;
our Englishmen laid on with their bowes
  as fast as they might dree.

The King of Scotts in a studye stood
  amongst his companye,
an arow stroke him thorrow the nose
  and thorrow his armorye.

The King went to a marsh side
  & light beside his steede,
and leaned him down on his sword hilt,
  to let his nose bleede.

there followed him a yeoman of merry England,
  his name was John of Coplande ;
" yield thee Traytor ! " cries Coplande then,
  " thy liffe lyes in my hand."

" how shold I yeeld me ? " sayes the King,
  " & thou art noe gentleman."
" Noe, by my troth," sayes Copland there,
  " I am but a poore yeoman ;

" What art thou better than I, Sir King ?
  tell me if that thou can !
What art thou better than I, Sir King ?
  now we be but man to man ? "

the King smote angerly at Copland then,
  angerly in that stonde ;
& then Copland was a bold yeoman,
  & bore the King to the ground.

He sett the King upon a Palfrey,
  himselfe upon a steede,
he tooke him by the bridle rayne,
  towards London he gan him Lead.

& when to London that he came,
  the King from ffrance was new come home,
& there unto the King of Scottes,
  he sayd these words anon.

"how like you my shepards & my millers,
  my priests with shaven crownes?"
"by my fayth, they are the sorest fighting men
  that ever I mett on the ground;

"there was never a yeoman in merry England
  but he was worth a Scottish knight!"
" I, by my troth," said King Edward, and laughe,
  "for you fought all against the right."

but now the Prince of merry England
  worthilye under his Sheelde
hath taken the King of ffrance
  at Poytiers in the ffeelde.

the Prince did present his father with that feod,
  the lovely King off ffrance,
& fforward of his Journey he is gone :
  god send us all good chance !

Thus ends the battell of ffaire Durham
  in one morning of may,
the battell of Cressey, & the battle of Potyers,
  All within one monthes day.

then was welthe and welfare in mery England,
  Solaces, game, & glee,
& every man loved other well,
  & the King loved good yeomanrye.

but God that made the grasse to growe,
  & leaves on greenwoode tree,
now save & keepe our noble King,
  & maintaine good yeomanrye !

Old Bailad.

———✦———

X.

THE ANCIENT BALLAD OF CHEVY-CHASE.

THE Percy out of Northumberland,
  And a vow to God made he,
That he would hunt in the mountains
  Of Cheviat within days three,
In the mauger of doughty Douglas,
  And all that ever with him be.

The fattest harts in all Cheviat
   He said he would kill, and carry them away :
" By my faith," said the doughty Douglas again,
   " I will let that hunting if that I may."

Then the Percy out of Bamborough came,
   With him a mighty meany ;
With fifteen hundred archers bold ;
   They were chosen out of shires three.

This began on a Monday at morn
   In Cheviat the hills so he ;
The child may rue that is unborn,
   It was the more pity.

The drivers thorough the woodes went
   For to rouse the deer ;
Bowmen bickarte upon the bent
   With their broad arrows clear.

They began in Cheviat the hills above
   Early on a Monynday :
By that it drew to the hour of noon
   A hundred fat harts dead there lay.

They blew a mort upon the bent,
   They 'sembled on sides sheer ;
To the quarry then the Percy went,
   To see the brittling of the deer.

He said, "It was the Douglas' promise
  This day to meet me here ;
But I wist he would fail verament :"
  A great oath the Percy sware.

At the last a squire of Northumberland
  Looked at his hand full nigh,
He was ware o' the doughty Douglas coming :
  With him a mighty meany.

Both with spear, bill, and brand :
  It was a mighty sight to see.
Hardier men both of heart nor hand
  Were not in Christianity.

They were twenty hundred spearmen good,
  Withouten any fail :
They were born along by the water of Tweed
  I' th' bounds of Tividale.

"Leave off the brittling of the deer," he said,
  "And to your bows look ye take good heed :
For never sith ye were on your mothers born,
  Had ye never so mickle need."

The doughty Douglas on a steed
  He rode at his men beforne ;
His armour glittered as did a glede,
  A bolder bairn was never born.

" Tell me what men ye are," he says,
  " Or whose men that ye be :
Who gave you leave to hunt in this
  Cheviat chase in the spite of me ? "

The first man that ever him an answer made,
  It was the good lord Percy :
" We will not tell thee what men we are," he says,
  " Nor whose men that we be :
But we will hunt here in this chase
  In the spite of thine and of thee.

" The fattest harts in all Cheviat
  We have kill'd, and cast to carry them away."
" By my troth," said the doughty Douglas again,
  " Therefor the one of us shall die this day."

Then said the doughty Douglas
  Unto the lord Percy :
" To kill all these guiltless men,
  Alas ! it were great pity.

" But, Percy, thou art a lord of land,
  I am an Earl called within my country ;
Let all our men upon a party stand ;
  And do the battle of thee and of me."

" Now Christ's curse on his crown," said the lord
    Percy,
  " Whosoever thereto says nay ;

By my troth, doughty Douglas," he says,
"Thou shalt never see that day;

"Neither in England, Scotland, nor France
Nor for no man of a woman born,
But an fortune be my chance,
I dare meet him one man for one."

Then bespake a squire of Northumberland—
Richard Witharington was his name;
"It shall never be told in South England," he says,
"To king Harry the Fourth for shame.

"I wot you bin great lordes twa,
I am a poor squire of land;
I will never see my captain fight on a field,
And stand myself and look on;
But while I may my weapons wield,
I will not fail, both heart and hand."

The English men had their bows y-bent,
Their hearts were good enow;
The first of arrows that they shot off,
Seven score spearmen they slew.

The Douglas parted his host in three,
Like a chief chieftain of pride;
With sure spears of mighty tree
They came in on every side.

The English men let their bows be,
  And pull'd out brands that were bright ;
It was a heavy sight to see
  Bright swords on basnets light.

At last the Douglas and the Percy met,
  Like two captains of might and main ;
They swapte together, till they both swat,
  With swords that were of fine Milàn.

These worthy freckys for to fight
  Thereto they were full fain,
Till the blood out of their basnets sprent,
  As ever did hail or rain.

"Hold thee, Percy," said the Douglas,
  "And, i' faith, I shall thee bring
Where thou shalt have an Earl's wages
  Of Jamy our Scottish King.

"Thou shalt have thy ransom free,
  I hight thee here this thing,
For the manfullest man yet art thou,
  That ever I conquer'd in field fighting."

"Nay," then said the lord Percy,
  "I told it thee beforne,
That I would never yielded be
  To no man of a woman born."

With that there came an arrow hastily
  Forth of a mighty one,
It hath stricken the Earl Douglas
  In at the breast-bone.

Thorough liver and lungs both
  The sharp arrow is gone,
That never after, in all his life days,
  He spake more words but one,
That was, "Fight ye, my merry men, whiles ye may,
  For my life days ben gone."

The Percy leaned on his brand,
  And saw the Douglas de;
He took the dead man by the hand,
  And said, "Woe is me for thee !

"To have saved thy life I would have parted with
  My lands for years three,
For a better man of heart nor of hand
  Was not in all the north country."

Of all that see, a Scottish knight,—
  Was called Sir Hugh the Mongon-byrry,—
He saw the Douglas to the death was dight;
  He spendyd a spear, a trusty tree :

He rode upon a corsiare
  Thorough a hundred archery;

He never stinted, nor never blane,
  Till he came to the good lord Percỳ.

He set upon the lord Percy
  A dint, that was full sore ;
With a sure spear of a mighty tree
  Clean thorough the body he the Percy bore.

At the t'other side, that a man might see,
  A large cloth yard and mare :
Two better captains were not in Christianty
  Than that day slain were there.

An archer of Northumberland.
  Saw slain was the lord Percỳ,
He bare a bent bow in his hand,
  Was made of trusty tree :

An arrow, that a cloth-yard was long,
  To th' hard steel haled he ;
A dint, that was both sad and sore,
  He set on Sir Hugh the Mongon-byrry.

The dint it was both sad and sore
  That he on Mongon-byrry set ;
The swan-feathers, that his arrow bore,
  With his heart blood they were wet.

There was never a freake one foot would flee,
  But still in stour did stand,

Hewing on each other while they might dre,
With many a baleful brand.

This battle began in Cheviat
An hour before the noon,
And when evensong bell was rung,
The battle was not half done.

They took on on either hand
By the light of the moon ;
Many had no strength for to stand
In Cheviat the hills aboon.

Of fifteen hundred archers of England
Went away but fifty and three :
Of twenty hundred spearmen of Scotland
But even five and fifty.

But all were slain Cheviat within ;
They had no strength to stand on hie
The child may rue, that is unborn,
It was the more pity.

There was slain with the lord Percy,
Sir John of Agerstone,
Sir Roger the hinde Hartly,
Sir William the bold Hearone.

Sir George the worthy Lovele,
A Knight of great renown,

Sir Raff the rich Rugby,
  With dints were beaten down.

For Witharington my heart was woe,
  That ever he slain should be :
For when both his legs were hewn in two,
  Yet he kneel'd and fought on his knee.

There was slain with the doughty Douglas
  Sir Hugh the Mongon-byrry,
Sir Davy Lwdale, that worthy was,—
  His sister's son was he :

Sir Charles a Murray, in that place,
  That never a foot would flee ;
Sir Hugh Maxwell, a lord he was,
  With the Douglas did he de.

So on the morrow they made them biers
  Of birch and hazel so gray ;
Many widows with weeping tears
  Came to fetch their mates away.

Tividale may carpe of care,
  Northumberland may make great moan :
For two such captains as slain were there
  On the march party shall never be none.

Word is comen to Edin-burrow
  To Jamy our Scottish King,

That doughty Douglas, lieutenant of the marches,
   He lay slain Cheviat within.

His hands did he weal and wring,
   He said, " Alas ! and woe is me !
Such another captain Scotland within,"
   He said, "i' faith should never be."

Word is comen to lovely London
   To the fourth Harry our king,
That Lord Percy, lieutenant of the marches,
   He lay slain Cheviat within.

" God have mercy on his soul," said King Harry,
   " Good Lord, if thy will it be !
I have a hundred captains in England," he said,
   " As good as ever was he :
But Percy, an I brook my life,
   Thy death well quit shall be."

As our noble king made his a-vow,
   Like a noble prince of renown,
For the death of the Lord Percy,
   He did the battle of Hombyll-down,

Where six and thirty Scottish knights
   On a day were beaten down :
Glendale glitter'd on their armour bright,
   Over castle, tower and town.

    *   *   *   *   *   *

Jesu Christ our balys bete
And to the bliss us bring !
Thus was the hunting of the Cheviat :
God send us all good ending !

Unknown.

— ++ —

XI.

THE GLORY OF ENGLAND—IN ECLIPSE.

Speech of John of Gaunt.

METHINKS I am a prophet new inspired—

＊　　＊　　＊　　＊　　＊　　＊

This royal throne of kings, this scepter'd isle,
This earth of majesty, this seat of Mars,
This other Eden, demi-paradise,
This fortress built by Nature for herself
Against infection and the hand of war ;
This happy breed of men, this little world,
This precious stone set in the silver sea,
Which serves it in the office of a wall,
Or as a moat defensive to a house,
Against the envy of less happier lands ;
This blessed plot, this earth, this realm, this England,
This nurse, this teeming womb of royal kings,
Fear'd by their breed and famous by their birth,

Renowned for their deeds as far from home,
For Christian service and true chivalry,
As is the sepulchre in stubborn Jewry
Of the world's ransom, blessed Mary's Son;
This land of such dear souls, this dear dear land,
Dear for her reputation thro' the world,
Is now leased out —I die pronouncing it—
Like to a tenement or pelting farm :
England, bound in with the triumphant sea,
Whose rocky shore beats back the envious siege
Of watery Neptune, is now bound in with shame,
With inky blots and rotten parchment bonds ;
That England, that was wont to conquer others,
Hath made a shameful conquest of itself.
Ah, would the scandal vanish with my life,
How happy then were my ensuing death !

SHAKSPERE, *King Richard II.*, Act ii. Sc. 1.

XII.

PRINCE HENRY OF MONMOUTH.

King Henry IV. But wherefore do I tell these news
to thee?
Why, Harry, do I tell thee of my foes,
Which art my near'st and dearest enemy ?

*　　*　　*　　*　　*　　*

Prince Henry. Do not think so ; you shall not find
   it so :
And God forgive them that so much have sway'd
Your majesty's good thoughts away from me !
I will redeem all this on Percy's head,
And, in the closing of some glorious day,
Be bold to tell you that I am your son ;
When I will wear a garment all of blood,
And stain my favours in a bloody mask,
Which, wash'd away, shall scour my shame with it :
And that shall be the day, whene'er it lights,
That this same child of honour and renown,
This gallant Hotspur, this all-praised knight,
And your unthought-of Harry chance to meet.
For every honour sitting on his helm,
Would they were multitudes, and on my head
My shames redoubled ! for the time will come,
That I shall make this northern youth exchange
His glorious deeds for my indignities.

　　*　　　*　　　*　　　*　　　*　　　*

This, in the name of God, I promise here ;
The which, if He be pleased I shall perform,
I do beseech your majesty may salve
The long-grown wounds of my intemperance :
If not, the end of life cancels all bands ;
And I will die a hundred thousand deaths,
Ere break the smallest parcel of this vow.

SHAKSPERE, 1 *Henry IV.*, Act iii. Sc. 2.

XIII.

THE TWO HARRYS.

Hotspur. He shall be welcome too. Where is his
    son,
The nimble-footed madcap Prince of Wales,
And his comrades, that daff'd the world aside,
And bid it pass?
    Vernon.   All furnish'd, all in arms :
All plumed like estridges, that with the wind
Bated,—like eagles having lately bathed ;
Glittering in golden coats, like images ;
As full of spirit as the month of May,
And gorgeous as the sun at midsummer ;
Wanton as youthful goats, wild as young bulls.
I saw young Harry, with his beaver on,
His cuisses on his thighs, gallantly arm'd,
Rise from the ground like feather'd Mercury,
And vaulted with such ease into his seat,   .
As if an angel dropp'd down from the clouds,
To turn and wind a fiery Pegasus,
And witch the world with noble horsemanship.
    Hotspur. No more, no more ; worse than the sun
    in March,
This praise doth nourish agues. Let them come ;
They come like sacrifices in their trim,
And to the fire-eyed maid of smoky war

All hot and bleeding will we offer them :
The mailed Mars shall on his altar sit,
Up to the ears in blood.   I am on fire,
To hear this rich reprisal is so nigh,
And yet not ours.   Come, let me taste my horse,
Who is to bear me like a thunderbolt
Against the bosom of the Prince of Wales :
Harry to Harry shall, hot horse to horse,
Meet, and ne'er part, till one drop down a corse.

SHAKSPERE, 1 *Henry IV.*, Act iv. Sc. 1.

XIV.

PRAISE OF AN ENEMY.

Prince. In both our armies there is many a soul
Shall pay full dearly for this encounter,
If once they join in trial.   Tell your nephew,
The Prince of Wales doth join with all the world
In praise of Henry Percy : by my hopes,
This present enterprise set off his head,
I do not think a braver gentleman,
More active-valiant or more valiant-young,
More daring or more bold, is now alive,
To grace this latter age with noble deeds.
For my part, I may speak it to my shame,
I have a truant been to chivalry ;

And so, I hear, he doth account me too;
Yet this before my father's majesty—
I am content that he should take the odds
Of his great name and estimation,
And will, to save the blood on either side,
Try fortune with him in a single fight.

    King. And, Prince of Wales, so dare we venture
    thee,
Albeit considerations infinite
Do make against it.—No, good Worcester, no,
We love our people well : even those we love
That are misled upon your cousin's part;
And, will they take the offer of our grace,
Both he and they and you, yea, every man
Shall be my friend again, and I'll be his :
So tell your cousin, and bring me word
What he will do : but if he will not yield,
Rebuke and dread correction wait on us,
And they shall do their office.   So, be gone;
We will not now be troubled with reply :
We offer fair ; take it advisedly.

                SHAKSPERE, 1 *Henry IV.*, Act v. Sc. 1.

XV.

A PRINCE INDEED.

Hotspur. O ! 'would the quarrel lay upon our heads,
And that no man might draw short breath to-day,
But I and Harry Monmouth ! Tell me, tell me,
How stood his tasking ? seem'd it in contempt ?
Vernon. No, by my soul : I never in my life
Did hear a challenge urged more modestly,
Unless a brother should a brother dare
To gentle exercise and proof of arms.
He gave you all the duties of a man ;
Trimm'd up your praises with a princely tongue,
Spoke your deservings like a chronicle,
Making you ever better than his praise,
By still dispraising praise, valued with you ;
And, which became him like a prince indeed,
He made a blushing cital of himself,
And chid his truant youth with such a grace,
As if he master'd there a double spirit
Of teaching and of learning instantly.
There did he pause : but let me tell the world,—
If he outlive the envy of this day,
England did never owe so sweet a hope,
So much misconstrued in his wantonness.

SHAKSPERE, 1 *Henry IV.*, Act v. Sc. 2.

XVI.

THE COURTEOUS VICTOR.

Hotspur. O Harry, thou hast robb'd me of my
   youth !
I better brook the loss of brittle life,
Than those proud titles thou hast won of me ;
They wound my thoughts worse than thy sword my
   flesh :
But thought's the slave of life, and life time's fool ;
And time, that takes survey of all the world,
Must have a stop.   O ! I could prophesy,
But that the earthy and cold hand of death
Lies on my tongue : no, Percy, thou art dust,
And food for——   [*Dies.*
   Prince. For worms, brave Percy.   Fare thee well,
      great heart !
Ill-weaved ambition, how much art thou shrunk !
When that this body did contain a spirit,
A kingdom for it was too small a bound ;
But now, two paces of the vilest earth
Is room enough : this earth, that bears thee dead,
Bears not alive so stout a gentleman.
If thou wert sensible of courtesy,
I should not make so dear a show of zeal :
But let my favours hide thy mangled face ;
And, even in thy behalf, I'll thank myself

For doing these fair rites of tenderness.
Adieu, and take thy praise with thee to heaven !
Thy ignomy sleep with thee in the grave,
But not remember'd in thy epitaph !

SHAKSPERE, 1 *Henry IV.*, Act v. Sc. 4.

———— ♦♦ ————

XVII.

REVERENCE FOR LAW.

King Henry V. You are right, justice, and you
weigh this well ;
Therefore still bear the balance and the sword :
And I do wish your honours may increase,
Till you do live to see a son of mine
Offend you, and obey you, as I did.
So shall I live to speak my father's words :
" Happy am I, that have a man so bold,
That dares do justice on my proper son ;
And not less happy, having such a son,
That would déliver up his greatness so
Into the hands of justice." You did commit me ;
For which I do commit into your hand
The unstain'd sword that you have used to bear ;
With this remembrance,—that you use the same
With the like bold, just and impartial spirit
As you have done 'gainst me. There is my hand.

You shall be as a father to my youth ;
My voice shall sound as you do prompt mine ear,
And I will stoop and humble my intents
To your well-practised, wise directions.
And, princes all, believe me, I beseech you :
My father is gone wild into his grave,
For in his tomb lie my affections ;
And with his spirit sadly I survive,
To mock the expectation of the world,
To frustrate prophecies, and to raze out
Rotten opinion, who hath writ me down
After my seeming. The tide of blood in me
Hath proudly flow'd in vanity till now :
Now doth it turn, and ebb back to the sea,
Where it shall mingle with the state of floods,
And flow henceforth in formal majesty.

SHAKSPERE, 2 *Henry IV.*, Act v. Sc. 2.

XVIII.

ENGLISHMEN IN THE FIELD.

King Henry V. (before Harfleur). Once more unto
    the breach, dear friends, once more ;
Or close the wall up with our English dead.
In peace there's nothing so becomes a man
As modest stillness and humility :

But, when the blast of war blows in our ears,
Then imitate the action of the tiger ;
Stiffen the sinews, summon up the blood,

＊   ＊   ＊   ＊   ＊   ＊

Then lend the eye a terrible aspect ;

＊   ＊   ＊   ＊   ＊   ＊

Hold hard the breath, and bend up every spirit
To his full height !—On, on, you noblest English,
Whose blood is fet from fathers of war-proof !
Fathers that, like so many Alexanders,
Have in these parts from morn till even fought,
And sheathed their swords for lack of argument.

＊   ＊   ＊   ＊   ＊   ＊

And you, good yeomen,
Whose limbs were made in England, show us here
The mettle of your pasture ; let us swear
That you are worth your breeding ; which I doubt
    not :
For there is none of you so mean and base,
That hath not noble lustre in your eyes.
I see you stand like greyhounds in the slips,
Straining upon the start. The game's afoot :
Follow your spirit, and upon this charge
Cry—" God for Harry ! England and Saint George ! "

SHAKSPERE, *King Henry V.*, Act iii. Sc. 1.

XIX

THE EVE OF ST. CRISPIAN.

THE poor condemned English,
Like sacrifices, by their watchful fires
Sit patiently, and inly ruminate
The morning's danger; and their gesture sad,
Investing lank-lean cheeks and war-worn coats,
Presenteth them unto the gazing moon
So many horrid ghosts.   O ! now, who will behold
The royal captain of this ruin'd band,
Walking from watch to watch, from tent to tent,
Let him cry—Praise and glory on his head !
For forth he goes, and visits all his host,
Bids them good-morrow with a modest smile,
And calls them brothers, friends, and countrymen.
Upon his royal face there is no note
How dread an army hath enrounded him ;
Nor doth he dedicate one jot of colour
Unto the weary and all-watched night :
But freshly looks, and overbears attaint
With cheerful semblance and sweet majesty ;
That every wretch, pining and pale before,
Beholding him, plucks comfort from his looks.
A largess universal, like the sun,
His liberal eye doth give to every one,

E

Thawing cold fear, that mean and gentle all
Behold, as may unworthiness define,
A little touch of Harry in the night.

Shakspere, *King Henry V.*, Act iv., Chorus.

XX.

HENRY THE FIFTH AND AGIN-COURT.

Westmoreland.   O ! that we now had here
But one ten thousand of those men in England
That do no work to-day !
King Henry.   What's he that wishes so ?
My cousin Westmoreland ?—No, my fair cousin :
If we are mark'd to die, we are enow
To do our country loss ; and if to live,
The fewer men the greater share of honour.
God's will ! I pray thee, wish not one man more.
By Jove, I am not covetous for gold,
Nor care I who doth feed upon my cost ;
It yearns me not if men my garments wear ;
Such outward things dwell not in my desires :
But, if it be a sin to covet honour,
I am the most offending soul alive.
No, 'faith, my coz, wish not a man from England :
God's peace ! I would not lose so great an honour,

As one man more, methinks, would share from me,
For the best hope I have. O, do not wish one more
Rather proclaim it, Westmoreland, thro' my host,
That he, which hath no stomach to this fight,—
Let him depart; his passport shall be made,
And crowns for convoy put into his purse :
We would not die in that man's company,
That fears his fellowship to die with us.
This day is call'd the feast of Crispian :
He that outlives this day, and comes safe home,
Will stand a tip-toe when this day is named,
And rouse him at the name of Crispian :
He that shall live this day, and see old age,
Will yearly on the vigil feast his neighbours,
And say, " To-morrow is Saint Crispian " :
Then will he strip his sleeve and show his scars,
And say, " These wounds I had on Crispin's day ".
Old men forget ; yet all shall be forgot,
But he'll remember with advantages
What feats he did that day : then shall our names,
Familiar in his mouth as household words,—
Harry the King, Bedford and Exeter,
Warwick and Talbot, Salisbury and Gloster,—
Be in their flowing cups freshly remember'd.
This story shall the good man teach his son ;
And Crispin Crispian shall ne'er go by,
From this day to the ending of the world,
But we in it shall be remembered ;

We few, we happy few, we band of brothers;
For he to-day that sheds his blood with me
Shall be my brother; be he ne'er so vile,
This day shall gentle his condition :
And gentlemen in England now a-bed
Shall think themselves accurst they were not here,
And hold their manhoods cheap whiles any speaks
That fought with us upon Saint Crispin's day.

SHAKSPERE, *King Henry V.,* Act iv. Sc. 3.

XXI.

BALLAD OF AGINCOURT.

FAIR stood the wind for France,
When we our sails advance,
Nor now to prove our chance
   Longer will tarry ;
But, putting to the main,
At Kaux, the mouth of Seine,
With all his martial train,
   Landed King Harry ;

And, taking many a fort
Furnish'd in warlike sort,
Marched towards Agincourt
   In happy hour,

Skirmishing day by day
With those that stopp'd his way,
Where the French General lay
    With all his power.

Which, in his height of pride
King Henry to deride,
His ransom to provide,
    To the King sending ;
Which he neglects the while,
As from a nation vile,
Yet, with an angry smile,
    Their fall portending.

And, turning to his men,
Quoth our brave Harry then,
" Though they be one to ten,
    Be not amazèd.
Yet have we well begun :—
Battles so bravely won
Have ever to the sun
    By fame been raisèd.

" And for myself," quoth he,
" This my full rest shall be ;
England ne'er mourn for me,
    Nor more esteem me :

Victor I will remain,
Or on this earth lie slain ;
Never shall she sustain
  Loss, to redeem me.

" Poitiers and Cressy tell,
When most their pride did swell,
Under our swords they fell :—
  No less our skill is,
Than when our Grandsire great,
Claiming the regal seat,
By many a warlike feat
  Lopp'd the French lilies."

The Duke of York so dread
The eager van-ward led ;
With the main Henry sped
  Amongst his henchmen ;
Excester had the rear,—
A braver man not there ;—
O Lord, how hot they were
  On the false Frenchmen !

They now to fight are gone :
Armour on armour shone ;
Drum now to drum did groan ;
  To hear was wonder ;

That with the cries they make
The very earth did shake ;
Trumpet to trumpet spake,
      Thunder to thunder.

Well it thine age became,
O noble Erpingham !
Which did the signal aim
      To our hid forces;
When, from a meadow by,
Like a storm, suddenly,
The English archery
      Struck the French horses

With Spanish yew so strong,
Arrows a cloth-yard long,
That like to serpents stung,
      Piercing the weather :
None from his fellow starts,
But, playing manly parts,
And like to English hearts,
      Stuck close together.

When down their bows they threw
And forth their bilboes drew,
And on the French they flew,
      Not one was tardy :

Arms were from shoulders sent,
Scalps to the teeth were rent,
Down the French peasants went :
    Our men were hardy.

This while, our noble King,
His broad sword brandishing,
Down the French host did ding,
    As to o'erwhelm it :
And many a deep wound lent,
His arms with blood besprent,
And many a cruel dent
    Bruisèd his helmet.

Gloster, that Duke so good,
Next of the royal blood,
For famous England stood
    With his brave brother ;
Clarence, in steel so bright,
Though but a maiden knight,
Yet in that furious fight
    Scarce such another.

Warwick in blood did wade,
Oxford the foe invade,
And cruel slaughter made
    Still, as they ran up ;

Suffolk his axe did ply;
Beaumont and Willoughby
Bare them right doughtily,
   Ferrers and Fanhope.

Upon Saint Crispin's day
Fought was this noble fray;
Which Fame did not delay
   T' England to carry:
O when shall Englishmen
With such acts fill a pen,
Or England breed again
   Such a King Harry?

       DRAYTON.

XXII.

FATHER AND SON.

The English Camp near Bordeaux.

Talbot. O young John Talbot! I did send for thee,
To tutor thee in stratagems of war,
That Talbot's name might be in thee revived,
When sapless age and weak unable limbs
Should bring thy father to his drooping-chair.
But,—O malignant and ill-boding stars!—

Now thou art come unto a feast of death,
A terrible and unavoided danger :
Therefore, dear boy, mount on my swiftest horse,
And I'll direct thee how thou shalt escape
By sudden flight : come, dally not, be gone.
    John. Is my name Talbot ? and am I your son ?
And shall I fly ?   O ! if you love my mother,
Dishonour not her honourable name,
To make a bastard and a slave of me :
The world will say, he is not Talbot's blood,
That basely fled, when noble Talbot stood.
    Talbot. Fly, to revenge my death, if I be slain.
    John. He that flies so will ne'er return again.
    Talbot. If we both stay, we both are sure to die.
    John. Then let me stay ; and, father, do you fly :
Your loss is great, so your regard should be ;
My worth unknown, no loss is known in me.
Upon my death the French can little boast ;
In yours they will, in you all hopes are lost.
Flight cannot stain the honour you have won ;
But mine it will, that no exploit have done :
You fled for vantage, every one will swear ;
But if I bow, they'll say it was for fear.
There is no hope that ever I will stay,
If the first hour I shrink and run away.
Here, on my knee, I beg mortality,
Rather than life preserved with infamy.

SHAKSPERE, 1 *Henry VI.*, Act iv. Sc. 5.

XXIII

RICHMOND AT BOSWORTH FIELD.

MORE than I have said, loving countrymen,
The leisure and enforcement of the time
Forbids to dwell on : yet remember this,—
God and our good cause fight upon our side :
The prayers of holy saints and wronged souls,
Like high-rear'd bulwarks, stand before our faces.
Richard except, those whom we fight against
Had rather have us win than him they follow.
For what is he they follow ? truly, gentlemen,
A bloody tyrant, and a homicide :
One raised in blood, and one in blood establish'd ;
One that made means to come by what he hath,
And slaughter'd those that were the means to help
      him :
A base, foul stone, made precious by the foil
Of England's chair, where he is falsely set :
One that hath ever been God's enemy.
Then, if you fight against God's enemy,
God will, in justice, ward you as his soldiers ;
If you do sweat to put a tyrant down,
You sleep in peace, the tyrant being slain ;
If you do fight against your country's foes,
Your country's fat shall pay your pains the hire ;
If you do fight in safeguard of your wives,

Your wives shall welcome home the conquerors;
If you do free your children from the sword,
Your children's children quit it in your age.—
Then, in the name of God and all these rights,
Advance your standards, draw your willing swords.
For me, the ransom of my bold attempt
Shall be this cold corse on the earth's cold face;
But if I thrive, the gain of my attempt,
The least of you shall share his part thereof.
Sound, drums and trumpets, boldly and cheerfully;
God and Saint George! Richmond and victory!

SHAKSPERE, *King Richard III.* Act v. Sc. 3.

———◆———

XXIV.

LATIMER AND RIDLEY: CRANMER.

Lord William Howard (afterwards Lord Howard, and Lord
    High Admiral).
Lord Paget.
Peters (Gentleman of Lord Howard).

Paget. And you saw Latimer and Ridley die?
Latimer was eighty, was he not? his best
Of life was over then.
Howard.   His eighty years
Look'd somewhat crooked on him in his frieze;
But after they had stript him to his shroud,

He stood upright, a lad of twenty-one,
And gather'd with his hands the starting flame,
And wash'd his hands and all his face therein,
Until the powder suddenly blew him dead.
Ridley was longer burning; but he died
As manfully and boldly, and, 'fore God,
I know them heretics, but right English ones.
If ever, as heaven grant, we clash with Spain,
Our Ridley-soldiers and our Latimer-sailors
Will teach her something.

    *   *   *   *   *   *

Peters, how pale you look ! you bring the smoke
Of Cranmer's burning with you.
    Peters.   Twice or thrice
The smoke of Cranmer's burning wrapt me round.
    Howard. Peters, you know me Catholic, but Eng-
    lish.
Did he die bravely ?   Tell me that, or leave
All else untold.
    Peters.   My Lord, he died most bravely.
    Howard. Then tell me all.
    Paget.   Ay, Master Peters, tell us.
    Peters. You saw him how he past among the
    crowd ;
And ever as he walk'd the Spanish friars
Still plied him with entreaty and reproach :
But Cranmer, as the helmsman at the helm
Steers, ever looking to the happy haven

Where he shall rest at night, moved to his death;
And I could see that many silent hands
Came from the crowd and met his own ; and thus,
When we had come where Ridley burnt with Latimer,
He, with a cheerful smile, as one whose mind
Is all made up, in haste put off the rags
They had mock'd his misery with, and all in white,
His long white beard, which he had never shaven
Since Henry s death, down-sweeping to the chain,
Wherewith they bound him to the stake, he stood
More like an ancient father of the Church
Than heretic of these times ; and still the friars
Plied him, but Cranmer only shook his head,
Or answer'd them in smiling negatives ;
Whereat Lord Williams gave a sudden cry :—
" Make short ! make short ! " and so they lit the wood.
Then Cranmer lifted his left hand to heaven,
And thrust his right into the bitter flame ;
And crying, in his deep voice, more than once,
" This hath offended—this unworthy hand ! "
So held it till it all was burn'd, before
The flame had reach'd his body; I stood near—
Mark'd him—he never utter'd moan of pain :
He never stirr'd or writhed, but, like a statue,
Unmoving in the greatness of the flame,
Gave up the ghost ; and so past martyr-like.

TENNYSON, *Queen Mary*, Act iv. Sc. 3.

XXV.

THE ARMADA.

ATTEND, all ye who list to hear our noble England's
  praise :
I tell of the thrice famous deeds she wrought in ancient
  days,
When that great fleet Invincible against her bore in
  vain
The richest spoils of Mexico, the stoutest hearts of
  Spain.

It was about the lovely close of a warm summer day,
There came a gallant merchant-ship full sail to Plymouth Bay ;
Her crew hath seen Castile's black fleet, beyond Aurigny's isle,
At earliest twilight, on the waves lie heaving many a
  mile.
At sunrise she escaped their van, by God's especial
  grace ;
And the tall Pinta, till the noon, had held her close in
  chase.

Forthwith a guard at every gun was placed along the
  wall ;
The beacon blazed upon the roof of Edgecumbe's
  lofty hall ;

Many a light fishing-bark put out to pry along the
coast,
And with loose rein and bloody spur rode inland many
a post.

With his white hair unbonneted, the stout old sheriff
comes ;
Behind him march the halberdiers ; before him sound
the drums ;
His yeomen round the market cross make clear an
ample space ;
For there behoves him to set up the standard of Her
Grace.
And haughtily the trumpets peal, and gaily dance the
bells,
As slow upon the labouring wind the royal blazon swells.

Look how the Lion of the sea lifts up his ancient crown
And underneath his deadly paw treads the gay lilies
down.
So stalk'd he when he turn'd to flight, on that famed
Picard field,
Bohemia's plume, and Genoa's bow, and Cæsar's eagle
shield.
So glared he when at Agincourt in wrath he turn'd to
bay,
And crush'd and torn beneath his claws the princely
hunters lay.

Ho ! strike the flagstaff deep, Sir Knight : ho ! scatter
  flowers, fair maids :
Ho ! gunners, fire a loud salute : ho ! gallants, draw
  your blades :
Thou sun, shine on her joyously ; ye breezes, waft her
  wide ;
Our glorious SEMPER EADEM, the banner of our pride.

The freshening breeze of eve unfurl'd that banner's
  massy fold ;
The parting gleam of sunshine kiss'd that haughty scroll
  of gold ;
Night sank upon the dusky beach, and on the purple
  sea ;
Such night in England ne'er had been, nor e'er again
  shall be.

From Eddystone to Berwick bounds, from Lynn to
  Milford Bay,
That time of slumber was as bright and busy as the
  day ;
For swift to east and swift to west the ghastly warflame
  spread,—
High on St. Michael's Mount it shone ; it shone on
  Beachy Head.
Far on the deep the Spaniard saw, along each southern
  shire,
Cape beyond cape, in endless range, those twinkling
  points of fire.

F

The fisher left his skiff to rock on Tamar's glittering
waves;

· The rugged miners pour'd to war from Mendip's
sunless caves;

O'er Longleat's towers, o'er Cranbourne's oaks, the
fiery herald flew :

He roused the shepherds of Stonehenge, the rangers
of Beaulieu.

Right sharp and quick the bells all night rang out
from Bristol town,

And ere the day three hundred horse had met on
Clifton down;

The sentinel on Whitehall gate look'd forth into the
night,

And saw o'erhanging Richmond Hill the streak of
blood-red light.

Then bugle's note and cannon's roar the deathlike
silence broke,

And with one start, and with one cry, the royal city woke.

At once on all her stately gates arose the answering
fires;

At once the wild alarum clash'd from all her reeling
spires;

From all the batteries of the Tower peal'd loud the
voice of fear;

And all the thousand masts of Thames sent back a
louder cheer :

And from the furthest wards was heard the rush of
hurrying feet,
And the broad streams of pikes and flags rush'd down
each roaring street;
And broader still became the blaze, and louder still
the din,
As fast from every village round the horse came
spurring in :
And eastward straight from wild Blackheath the war-
like errand went,
And roused in many an ancient hall the gallant
squires of Kent.
Southward from Surrey's pleasant hills flew those
bright couriers forth ;
High on bleak Hampstead's swarthy moor they started
for the north ;
And on, and on, without a pause, untired they
bounded still :
All night from tower to tower they sprang; they
sprang from hill to hill :
Till the proud Peak unfurl'd the flag o'er Darwin's
rocky dales,
Till like volcanoes flared to heaven the stormy hills of
Wales,
Till twelve fair counties saw the blaze on Malvern's
lonely height,
Till stream'd in crimson on the wind the Wrekin's
crest of light.

Till broad and fierce the star came forth on Ely's
stately fane,
And tower and hamlet rose in arms o'er all the bound-
less plain ;
Till Belvoir's lordly terraces the sign to Lincoln sent,
And Lincoln sped the message on o'er the wide vale
of Trent ;
Till Skiddaw saw. the fire that burned on Gaunt's em-
battled pile,
And the red glare on Skiddaw roused the burghers of
Carlisle.

* *   * * *

MACAULAY.

XXVI.

THE REVENGE: A BALLAD OF THE
FLEET.

I.

AT FLORES in the Azores Sir Richard Grenville lay,
And a pinnace, like a flutter'd bird, came flying from
far away :
"Spanish ships of war at sea ! we have sighted fifty-
three ! "
Then sware Lord Thomas Howard : " 'Fore God I
am no coward ;

But I cannot meet them here, for my ships are out of
  gear,
And the half my men are sick. I must fly, but
  follow quick.
We are six ships of the line ; can we fight with fifty-
  three ? "

II.

Then spake Sir Richard Grenville : " I know you are
  no coward ;
You fly them for a moment to fight with them again.
But I've ninety men and more that are lying sick
  ashore.   .
I should count myself the coward if I left them, my
  Lord Howard,
To these Inquisition dogs and the devildoms of Spain."

III.

So Lord Howard past away with five ships of war that
  day,   .
Till he melted like a cloud in the silent summer
  heaven ;
But Sir Richard bore in hand all his sick men from
  the land
Very carefully and slow,
Men of Bideford in Devon,
And we laid them on the ballast down below ;
For we brought them all aboard,

And they blest him in their pain, that they were not
    left to Spain,
To the thumbscrew and the stake, for the glory of the
    Lord.

IV.

He had only a hundred seamen to work the ship
    and to fight,
And he sailed away from Flores till the Spaniard came
    in sight,
With his huge sea-castles heaving upon the weather
    bow.
" Shall we fight or shall we fly ?
Good Sir Richard, tell us now,
For to fight is but to die !
There'll be little of us left by the time this sun be set.
And Sir Richard said again : " We be all good
    English men.
Let us bang these dogs of Seville, the children of the
    devil,
For I never turn'd my back upon Don or devil yet."

V.

Sir Richard spoke and he laugh'd, and we roar'd a
    hurrah, and so
The little Revenge ran on sheer into the heart of the
    foe,
With her hundred fighters on deck, and her ninety
    sick below ;

For half of their fleet to the right and half to the left
    were seen,
And the little Revenge ran on thro' the long sea-lane
    between.

VI.

Thousands of their soldiers look'd down from their
    decks and laugh'd,
Thousands of their seamen made mock at the mad
    little craft
Running on and on, till delay'd
By their mountain-like San Philip' that, of fifteen
    hundred tons,
And up-shadowing high above us with her yawning
    tiers of guns,
Took the breath from our sails, and we stay'd.

VII.

And while now the great San Philip hung above us
    like a cloud
Whence the thunderbolt will fall
Long and loud,
Four galleons drew away
From the Spanish fleet that day,
And two upon the larboard and two upon the star-
    board lay,
And the battle-thunder broke from them all.

VIII.

But anon the great San Philip, she bethought herself
and went
Having that within her womb that had left her ill
content ;
And the rest they came aboard us, and they fought
us hand to hand,
For a dozen times they came with their pikes and
musquetcers,
And a dozen times we shook 'em off as a dog that
shakes his ears
When he leaps from the water to the land.

IX.

And the sun went down, and the stars came out far
over the summer sea,
But never a moment ceased the fight of the one and
the fifty-three.
Ship after ship, the whole night long, their high-built
galleons came,
Ship after ship, the whole night long, with her battle-
thunder and flame ;
Ship after ship, the whole night long, drew back with
her dead and her shame.
For some were sunk and many were shatter'd, and so
could fight us no more—
God of battles, was ever a battle like this in the world
before ?

X.

For he said " Fight on ! fight on !"
Tho' his vessel was all but a wreck ;
And it chanced that, when half of the short summer
night was gone,
With a grisly wound to be drest he had left the deck,
But a bullet struck him that was dressing it suddenly
dead,
And himself he was wounded again in the side and
the head,
And he said " Fight on ! fight on !"

XI.

And the night went down, and the sun smiled out far
over the summer sea,
And the Spanish fleet with broken sides lay round us
all in a ring ;
But they dared not touch us again, for they fear'd that
we still could sting,
So they watch'd what the end would be.
And we had not fought them in vain,
But in perilous plight were we,
Seeing forty of our poor hundred were slain,
And half of the rest of us maim'd for life
In the crash of the cannonades and the desperate
strife ;

And the sick men down in the hold were most of
    them stark and cold,
And the pikes were all broken or bent, and the powder
    was all of it spent ;
And the masts and the rigging were lying over the side ;
But Sir Richard cried in his English pride,
" We have fought such a fight for a day and a night
As may never be fought again !
We have won great glory, my men !
And a day less or more
At sea or ashore,
We die—does it matter when ?
Sink me the ship, Master Gunner—sink her, spilt her
    in twain !
Fall into the hands of God, not into the hands of
    Spain ! ".

XII.

And the gunner said " Ay, ay," but the seamen made
    reply : '
" We have children, we have wives,
And the Lord hath spared our lives.
We will make the Spaniard promise, if we yield, to let
    us go ;
We shall live to fight again and to strike another blow."
And the lion there lay dying, and they yielded to the
    foe.

XIII.

And the stately Spanish men to their flagship bore
    him then,
Where they laid him by the mast, old Sir Richard
    caught at last,
And they praised him to his face with their courtly
    foreign grace ;
But he rose upon their decks, and he cried :
" I have fought˙ for Queen and Faith like a valiant
    man and true ;
I have only done my duty as a man is bound to do :
With a joyful spirit I Sir Richard Grenville die ! "
And he fell upon their decks, and he died.

XIV.

And they stared at the dead that had been so valiant
    and true,
And had holden the power and glory of Spain so
    cheap
That he dared her with one little ship and his English
    few ;
Was he devil or man ? He was devil for aught they
    knew,
But they sank his body with honour down into the
    deep,
And they mann'd the Revenge with a swarthier alien
    crew,

And away she sail'd with her loss and long'd for her
    own ;
When a wind from the lands they had ruin'd awoke
    from sleep,
And the water began to heave and the weather to
    moan,
And or ever that evening ended a great gale blew,
And a wave like the wave that is raised by an earth-
    quake grew,
Till it smote on their hulls and their sails and their
    masts and their flags,
And the whole sea plunged and fell on the shot-
    shatter'd navy of Spain,
And the little Revenge herself went down by the
    island crags
To be lost evermore in the main.

TENNYSON.

XXVII.

CROMWELL AND HAMPDEN.

UPON the pier stood two stern-visaged men,
Looking to where a little craft lay moor'd,
Sway'd by the lazy current of the Thames,
Which welter'd by in muddy listlessness.
Grave men they were, and battlings of fierce thought

Had trampled out all softness from their brows,
And plough'd rough furrows there before their time.
Care, not of self, but of the common weal,
Had robb'd their eyes of youth, and left instead
A look of patient power and iron will,
And something fiercer too, that gave broad hint
Of the plain weapons girded at their sides.

    *   *   *   *   *   *

"Hampden ! a moment since my purpose was
To fly with thee,—for I will call it flight,
Nor flatter it with any smoother name—
But something in me bids me not to go ; . . .
Why should we fly ?   Nay, why not rather stay
And rear again our Zion's crumbled walls,
Not, as of old the walls of Thebes were built,
With minstrel twanging, but, if need should be,
With the more potent music of our swords ?
Think'st thou that score of men beyond the sea
Claim more God's care than all of England here ? . . .
Believe it, 'tis the mass of men He loves ;
And where there is most sorrow and most want,
Where the high heart of man is trodden down
The most, 'tis not because He hides His face
From them in wrath, as purblind teachers prate ;—
Not so : there most is He, for there is He
Most needed.   Men who seek for Fate abroad
Are not so near His heart as they who dare
Frankly to face her where she faces them,

On their own threshold where their hearts are strong.
No, Hampden ! they have half-way conquer'd Fate
Who go half-way to meet her—as will I.
Freedom hath yet a work for me to do ;
So speaks that inward voice which never yet
Spake falsely, when it urged the spirit on
To noble deeds for country and mankind.
And, for success, I ask no more than this—
To bear unflinching witness to the truth.
All true, whole men succeed ; for what is worth
Success's name, unless it be the thought,
The inward surety to have carried out
A noble purpose to a noble end,
Although it be the gallows or the block ?
'Tis only Falsehood that doth ever need
Those outward shows of gain to bolster her.
Be it we prove the weaker with our swords ;
Truth only needs to be for once spoke out,
And there's such music in her, such strange rhythm,
As makes men's memories her joyous slaves,
And clings around the soul, as the sky clings
Round the mute earth, for ever beautiful,
And, if o'erclouded, only to burst forth
More all-embracingly divine and clear :
Get but the truth once utter'd, and 'tis like
A star new-born, that drops into its place,
And which, once circling in its placid round,
Not all the tumult of the earth can shake.

" New times demand new measures and new men ;
The world advances, and in time outgrows
The laws that in our fathers' day were best.
      *   *   *   *   *
Our time is one that calls for earnest deeds :
Reason and government, like two broad seas,
Yearn for each other with outstretched arms,
Across this narrow isthmus of the throne,
And roll their white surf higher every day.
      *   *   *   *   *
The time is ripe, and rotten-ripe, for change.
Then let it come : I have no dread of what
Is call'd for by the instinct of mankind ;
Nor think I that God's world will fall apart,
Because we tear a parchment more or less.
      *   *   *   *   *
He who would win the name of truly great
Must understand his own age and the next,
And make the present ready to fulfil
Its prophecy, and with the future merge
Gently and peacefully, as wave with wave.
      *   *   *   *   *
I do not fear to follow out the truth,
Albeit along the precipice's edge.
Let us speak plain : there is more force in names
Than most men dream of ; and a lie may keep
Its throne a whole age longer, if it skulk
Behind the shield of some fair-seeming name.
Let us call tyrants *tyrants*, and maintain

That only freedom comes by grace of God,
And all that comes not by His grace must fall ;
For men in earnest hɑve no time to waste,
In patching fig-leaves for the naked truth."

     *   *   *   *   *   ɑ

So they two turn'd together : one to die
Fighting for freedom on the battle-field ;
The other, far more happy, to become
A name earth wears for ever next her heart ;
One of the few that have a right to rank
With the true Makers : for his spirit wrought
Order from Chaos ; proved that right divine
Dwelt only in the excellence of truth ; .
And far within old Darkness' hostile lines
Advanced and pitch'd the shining tents of Light.

LOWELL.

XXVIII.

TO SIR HENRY VANE, THE YOUNGER.

VANE, young in years, but in sage counsel old,
Than whom a better senator ne'er held
The helm of Rome, when gowns, not arms, repell'd
The fierce Epirot and the African bold ;
Whether to settle peace, or to unfold
The drift of hollow states hard to be spell'd ;
Then to advise how War may, best upheld,
Move by her two main nerves, iron and gold

In all her equipage : besides to know
Both spiritual power and civil, what each means,
What severs each, thou hast learn'd, which few have
    done :
The bounds of either sword to thee we owe :   ˙
Therefore on thy firm hand Religion leans
In peace, and reckons thee her eldest son.

MILTON.

———◦———

XXIX.

TO THE LORD GENERAL FAIRFAX.

FAIRFAX, whose name in arms thro' Europe rings,
Filling each mouth with envy or with praise,
And all her jealous monarchs with amaze,
And rumours loud that daunt remotest kings :
Thy firm unshaken virtue ever brings
Victory home, tho' new rebellions raise
Their Hydra heads, and the false North displays
Her broken league to imp their serpent-wings.
O yet a nobler task awaits thy hand,
(For what can war but endless war still breed ?)
Till Truth and Right from violence be freed,
And Public Faith clear'd from the shameful brand
Of public fraud.   In vain doth Valour bleed,
While Avarice and Rapine share the land.

MILTON.

G

XXX.

CHATHAM AND WOLFE.

ENGLAND, with all thy faults, I love thee still,
My country ! and, while yet a nook is left
Where English minds and manners may be found,
Shall be constrain'd to love thee.

    *   *   *   *   *   *

To shake thy senate, and from heights sublime
Of patriot eloquence to flash down fire
Upon thy foes, was never meant my task ;
But I can feel thy fortunes, and partake
Thy joys and sorrows with as true a heart
As any thunderer there.   And I can feel
Thy follies too, and with a just disdain
Frown at effeminates, whose very looks
Reflect dishonour on the name I love.

    *   *   *   *   *   *

Time was when it was praise and boast enough
In every clime, and travel where we might,
That we were born her children ; praise enough
To fill the ambition of a private man,
That Chatham's language was his mother tongue,
And Wolfe's great name compatriot with his own
Farewell those honours, and farewell with them
The hope of such hereafter !   They have fallen
Each in his field of glory : one in arms,
And one in council—Wolfe upon the lap

Of smiling Victory that moment won,
And Chatham, heart-sick of his country's shame !
They made us many soldiers.   Chatham still
Consulting England's happiness at home,
Secured it by an unforgiving frown
If any wrong'd her.   Wolfe, where'er he fought,
Put so much of his heart into his act,
That his example had a magnet's force,
And all were swift to follow whom all loved.
Those suns are set.   O rise some other such !
Or all that we have left is empty talk
Of old achievements, and despair of new.

COWPER.

XXXI.
ENGLISH FREEDOM AND ENGLISH CHARACTER: A FALLING AWAY.

THEE I account still happy, and the chief
Among the nations, seeing thou art free,
My native nook of earth ! . . . [and] for the sake
Of that one feature can be well content,
Disgraced as thou hast been, poor as thou art,
To seek no sublunary rest beside.
But once enslaved, farewell ! I could endure
Chains nowhere patiently, and chains at home,
Where I am free by birthright, not at all.

    *   *   *   *   *   *

And if I must bewail the blessing lost,
For which our Hampdens and our Sidneys bled,
I would at least bewail it under skies
Milder, among a people less austere,
In scenes which, having never known me free,
Would not reproach me with the loss I felt.
Do I forbode impossible events,
And tremble at false dreams? Heaven grant I may!
But the age of virtuous politics is past,
And we are deep in that of cold pretence.
Patriots are grown too shrewd to be sincere,
And we too wise to trust them.

    *   *   *   *   *   *

For when was public virtue to be found
Where private was not? Can he love the whole
Who loves no part? He be a nation's friend,
Who is in truth the friend of no man there?
Can he be strenuous in his country's cause,
Who slights the charities, for whose dear sake
That country, if at all, must be beloved?

    *   *   *   *   *   *

Such were not they of old, whose temper'd blades
Dispersed the shackles of usurp'd control,
And hew'd them link from link. Then Albion's sons
Were sons indeed; they felt a filial heart
Beat high within them at a mother's wrongs,
And, shining each in his domestic sphere,
Shone brighter still, once call'd to public view.

COWPER.

XXXII.

BATTLE OF THE BALTIC.

Of Nelson and the North
Sing the glorious day's renown
When to battle fierce came forth
All the might of Denmark's crown,
And her arms along the deep proudly shone ;
By each gun the lighted brand
In a bold determined hand,
And the Prince of all the land
Led them on.

Like leviathans afloat
Lay their bulwarks on the brine ;
While the sign of battle flew
On the lofty British line :
It was ten of April morn by the chime :
As they drifted on their path,
There was silence deep as death ;
And the boldest held their breath
For a time.

But the might of England flush'd
To anticipate the scene ;
And her van the fleeter rush'd
O'er the deadly space between.

"Hearts of oak!" our captains cried, when each gun
From its adamantine lips
Spread a death-shade round the ships,
Like the hurricane eclipse
Of the sun.

Again ! again ! again !
And the havoc did not slack,
Till a feeble cheer the Dane
To our cheering sent us back ;—
Their shots along the deep slowly boom :—
Then ceased—and all is wail,
As they strike the shatter'd sail ;
Or in conflagration pale
Light the gloom.

Out spoke the victor then,
As he hail'd them o'er the wave,
" Ye are brothers ! ye are men !
And we conquer but to save :—
So peace instead of death let us bring :
But yield, proud foe, thy fleet
With the crews, at England's feet,
And make submission meet
To our King."

Then Denmark blest our chief
That he gave her wounds repose ;

And the sounds of joy and grief
From her people wildly rose,
As death withdrew his shades from the day :
While the sun look'd smiling bright
O'er a wide and woeful sight,
Where the fires of funeral light
Died away.

Now joy, old England, raise,
For the tidings of thy might,
By the festal cities' blaze,
Whilst the wine-cup shines in light ;
And yet amidst that joy and uproar,
Let us think of them that sleep
Full many a fathom deep
By thy wild and stormy steep
Elsinore !

Brave hearts ! to Britain's pride
Once so faithful and so true,
On the deck of fame that died
With the gallant good Riou :
Soft sigh the winds of heaven o'er their grave !
While the billow mournful rolls
And the mermaid's song condoles
Singing glory to the souls
Of the brave !

CAMPBELL.

XXXIII.

"MILTON! THOU SHOULDST BE LIVING."

MILTON! thou shouldst be living at this hour :
England hath need of thee : she is a fen
Of stagnant waters : altar, sword, and pen,
Fireside, the heroic wealth of hall and bower
Have forfeited their ancient English dower
Of inward happiness.   We are selfish men ;
O ! raise us up, return to us again ;
And give us manners, virtue, freedom, power.
Thy soul was like a Star, and dwelt apart :
Thou hadst a voice whose sound was like the sea ;
Pure as the naked heavens, majestic, free ;
So didst thou travel on life's common way,
In cheerful godliness ; and yet thy heart
The lowliest duties on itself did lay.

WORDSWORTH.

XXXIV.

THE HERITAGE OF ENGLISHMEN.

IT is not to be thought of that the flood
Of British freedom, which, to the open sea
Of the world's praise, from dark antiquity

Hath flow'd, " with pomp of waters unwithstood,"—
Road by which all might come and go that would,
And bear out freights of worth to foreign lands ;
That this most famous stream in bogs and sands
Should perish, and to evil and to good
Be lost for ever.   In our halls is hung
Armoury of the invincible Knights of old :
We must be free or die, who speak the tongue
That Shakspere spake—the faith and morals hold
Which Milton held.   In everything we are sprung
Of Earth's first blood, have titles manifold.

WORDSWORTH.

XXXV.

A PATRIOT'S FEARS.

WHEN I have borne in memory what has tamed
Great nations, how ennobling thoughts depart,
When men change swords for ledgers, and desert
The student's bower for gold, some fears unnamed
I had, my Country !—am I to be blamed ?
But when I think of thee, and what thou art,
Verily, in the bottom of my heart,
Of those unfilial fears I am ashamed.
For dearly must we prize thee ; we who find
In thee a bulwark of the cause of men ;

And I by my affection was beguiled :
What wonder if a Poet now and then,
Among the many movements of his mind
Felt for thee as a lover or a child !

WORDSWORTH.

———— ♦ ————

XXXVI.

TO THE MEN OF KENT.

October, 1803

VANGUARD of liberty, ye men of Kent !
Ye children of a Soil that doth advance
Her haughty brow against the coast of France,
Now is the time to prove your hardiment !
To France be words of invitation sent !
They from their fields can see the countenance
Of your fierce war, may ken the glittering lance,
And hear you shouting forth your brave intent.
Left single, in bold parley, ye, of yore,
Did from the Norman win a gallant wreath :
Confirm'd the charters that were yours before.
No parleying now ! In Britain is one breath ;
We all are with you now from shore to shore :
Ye men of Kent, 'tis victory or death !

WORDSWORTH.

XXXVII.

BUONAPARTE.

HE thought to quell the stubborn hearts of oak,
Madman !—to chain with chains and bind with bands
That island queen who sways the floods and lands
From Ind to Ind,—but in fair daylight woke,
When from her wooden walls, lit by sure hands,
With thunders and with lightnings and with smoke,
Peal after peal, the British battle broke,
Lulling the brine against the Coptic sands.
We taught him lowlier moods, when Elsinore
Heard the war moan along the distant sea,
Rocking with shatter'd spars, with sudden fires
Flamed over : at Trafalgar yet once more
We taught him : late he learn'd humility
Perforce, like those whom Gideon school'd with briers.

TENNYSON.

————◦◦————

XXXVIII.

CHARACTER OF THE HAPPY WARRIOR.

WHO is the Happy Warrior? Who is he
That every man in arms should wish to be ?
—It is the generous Spirit, who, when brought
Among the tasks of real life, hath wrought

Upon the plan that pleased his childish thought :
Whose high endeavours are an inward light
That makes the path before him always bright :
Who, with a natural instinct to discern
What knowledge can perform, is diligent to learn ;
Abides by this resolve, and stops not there,
But makes his moral being his prime care :
Who, doom'd to go in company with Pain,
And Fear, and Bloodshed,—miserable train !—
Turns his necessity to glorious gain ;
In face of these doth exercise a power,
Which is our human nature's highest dower ;
Controls them and subdues, transmutes, bereaves
Of their bad influence, and their good receives ;
By objects, which might force the soul to abate
Her feeling, render'd more compassionate ;
Is placable,—because occasions rise
So often that demand such sacrifice ;
More skilful in self-knowledge, even more pure,
As tempted more ; more able to endure,
As more exposed to suffering and distress ;
Thence, also, more alive to tenderness.
—'Tis he whose law is reason ; who depends
Upon that law as on the best of friends ;
Whence, in a state where men are tempted still
To evil for a guard against worse ill,
And what in quality or act is best
Doth seldom on a right foundation rest,

He fixes good on good alone, and owes
To virtue every triumph that he knows :
—Who, if he rise to station of command,
Rises by open means, and there will stand
On honourable terms, or else retire,
And in himself possess his own desire :
Who comprehends his trust, and to the same
Keeps faithful with a singleness of aim ;
And therefore does not stoop, nor lie in wait
For wealth, or honours, or for worldly state ;
Whom they must follow ; on whose head must fall
Like showers of manna, if they come at all :
Whose powers shed round him in the common strife,
Or mild concerns of ordinary life,
A constant influence, a peculiar grace ;
But who, if he be call'd upon to face
Some awful moment, to which Heaven has join'd
Great issues, good or bad for human kind,
Is happy as a lover, and attired
With sudden brightness, like a man inspired ;
And, through the heat of conflict, keeps the law
In calmness made, and sees what he foresaw ;
Or, if an unexpected call succeed,
Come when it will, is equal to the need :
—He who, though thus endued as with a sense
And faculty for storm and turbulence,
Is yet a soul whose master-bias leans
To home-felt pleasures and to gentle scenes ;

Sweet images ! which, wheresoe'er he be,
Are at his heart ; and such fidelity
It is his darling passion to approve;
More brave for this, that he hath much to love :
—'Tis, finally, the man, who, lifted high,
Conspicuous object in a nation's eye,
Or left unthought-of in obscurity,—
Who, with a toward or untoward lot,
Prosperous or adverse, to his wish or not,
Plays, in the many games of life, that one
Where what he most doth value must be won ;
Whom neither shape of danger can dismay,
Nor thought of tender happiness betray :
Who, not content that former worth stand fast,
Looks forward, persevering to the last,
From well to better, daily self-surpass'd :
Who, whether praise of him must walk the earth
For ever, and to noble deeds give birth,
Or he must go to dust without his fame,
And leave a dead, unprofitable name,
Finds comfort in himself and in his cause ;
And, while the mortal mist is gathering, draws
His breath in confidence of Heaven's applause.
—This is the Happy Warrior ; this is he
That every man in arms should wish to be.

WORDSWORTH.

XXXIX.

"YE MARINERS OF ENGLAND."

YE Mariners of England,
That guard our native seas !
Whose flag has braved, a thousand years,
The battle and the breeze !
Your glorious standard launch again
To match another foe :
And sweep through the deep,
While the stormy winds do blow ;
While the battle rages loud and long,
And the stormy winds do blow.

The spirits of your fathers
Shall start from every wave,—
For the deck it was their field of fame,
And Ocean was their grave :
Where Blake and mighty Nelson fell
Your manly hearts shall glow,
As ye sweep through the deep,
While the stormy winds do blow ;
While the battle rages loud and long,
And the stormy winds do blow.

Britannia needs no bulwarks,
No towers along the steep ;

Her march is o'er the mountain waves,
Her home is on the deep.
With thunders from her native oak
She quells the floods below—
As they roar on the shore,
When the stormy winds do blow;
When the battle rages loud and long,
And the stormy winds do blow.

The meteor flag of England
Shall yet terrific burn;
Till danger's troubled night depart,
And the star of peace return.
Then, then, ye ocean-warriors!
Our song and feast shall flow
To the fame of your name,
When the storm has ceased to blow;
When the fiery fight is heard no more,
And the storm has ceased to blow.

CAMPBELL.

XL.

TO WILLIAM WILBERFORCE, ESQ.

THY country, Wilberforce, with just disdain
Hears thee by cruel men and impious call'd
Fanatic, for thy zeal to loose the enthrall'd
From exile, public sale, and slavery's chain.
Friend of the poor, the wrong'd, the fetter-gall'd,
Fear not lest labour such as thine be vain !
Thou hast achieved a part ; hast gain'd the ear
Of Britain's senate to thy glorious cause.
Hope smiles, joy springs, and tho' cold caution pause
And weave delay, the better hour is near,
That shall remunerate thy toils severe
By peace for Afric, fenced with British laws.
Enjoy what thou hast won, esteem and love
From all the just on earth and all the blest above.

COWPER.

April 16, 1792.

XLI.

TO THOMAS CLARKSON,

On the Final Passing of the Bill for the Abolition
of the Slave Trade, March, 1807.

CLARKSON ! it was an obstinate hill to climb :
How toilsome, nay, how dire it was, by thee .
Is known—by none, perhaps, so feelingly :
But thou, who, starting in thy fervent prime,
Didst first lead forth this pilgrimage sublime,
Hast heard the constant Voice its charge repeat,
Which, out of thy young heart's oracular seat,
First roused thee.—O true yoke-fellow of Time,
Duty's intrepid liegeman, see, the palm
Is won, and by all nations shall be worn !
The bloody writing is for ever torn ;
And thou henceforth shalt have a good man's calm,
A great man's happiness ; thy zeal shall find
Repose at length, firm friend of human kind !

WORDSWORTH.

XLII.

ARNOLD OF RUGBY.

*   *   *   *   *

O STRONG soul, by what shore
Tarriest thou now? For that force,
Surely, has not been left vain!
Somewhere, surely, afar,
In the sounding labour-house vast
Of being, is practised that strength,
Zealous, beneficent, firm!

Yes, in some far-shining sphere,
Conscious or not of the past,
Still thou performest the word
Of the Spirit in whom thou dost live—
Prompt, unwearied, as here!
Still thou upraisest with zeal
The humble good from the ground,
Sternly repressest the bad!
Still, like a trumpet, dost rouse
Those who with half-open eyes
Tread the border-land dim
'Twixt vice and virtue; reviv'st,
Succourest!—this was thy work,
This was thy life upon earth.

*   *   *   *   *

We were weary, and we .
Fearful, and we, in our march,
Fain to drop down and to die.
Still thou turnedst, and still
Beckonedst the trembler, and still
Gavest the weary thy hand !
If, in the paths of the world,
Stones might have wounded thy feet,
Toil or dejection have tried
Thy spirit, of that we saw
Nothing ! to us thou wert still
Cheerful, and helpful, and firm.
Therefore to thee it was given
Many to save with thyself ;
And, at the end of thy day,
O faithful shepherd ! to come,
Bringing thy sheep in thy hand.

And through thee I believe
In the noble and great who are gone ;
Pure souls honour'd and blest
By former ages, who else—
Such, so soulless, so poor,
Is the race of men whom I see—
Seem'd but a dream of the heart,
Seem'd but a cry of desire.
Yes ! I believe that there lived
Others like thee in the past,

Not like the men of the crowd
Who all round me to-day
Bluster or cringe, and make life
Hideous, and arid, and vile ;
But souls temper'd with fire,
Fervent, heroic, and good,
Helpers and friends of mankind.

Servants of God !—or sons
Shall I not call you ? because
Not as servants ye knew
Your Father's innermost mind,
His, who unwillingly sees
One of his little ones lost—
Yours is the praise, if mankind
Hath not as yet in its march
Fainted, and fallen, and died !

See ! in the rocks of the world
Marches the host of mankind,
A feeble, wavering line !
Where are they tending ?—A God
Marshall'd them, gave them their goal.—
Ah, but the way is so long !
Years they have been in the wild !
Sore thirst plagues them ; the rocks,
Rising all round, overawe.
Factions divide them—their host
Threatens to break, to dissolve.—

Ah, keep, keep them combined !
Else, of the myriads who fill
That army, not one shall arrive !
Sole they shall stray ; in the rocks
Labour for ever in vain,
Die one by one in the waste.

Then, in such hour of need
Of your fainting, dispirited race,
Ye, like angels, appear,
Radiant with ardour divine.
Beacons of hope, ye appear !
Languor is not in your heart,
Weakness is not in your word,
Weariness not on your brow.
Ye alight in our van ! at your voice,
Panic, despair, flee away.
Ye move through the ranks, recall
The stragglers, refresh the outworn,
Praise, re-inspire the brave !
Order, courage, return ;
Eyes rekindling, and prayers,
Follow your steps as ye go.
Ye fill up the gaps in our files,
Strengthen the wavering line,
Stablish, continue our march,
On, to the bound of the waste,
On, to the City of God !

MATTHEW ARNOLD.

XLIII.

ODE ON THE DEATH OF THE DUKE OF WELLINGTON.

I.

BURY the Great Duke
With an empire's lamentation,
Let us bury the Great Duke
To the noise of the mourning of a mighty nation,—
Mourning when their leaders fall,
Warriors carry the warrior's pall,
And sorrow darkens hamlet and hall.

II.

Where shall we lay the man whom we deplore?
Here, in streaming London's central roar.
Let the sound of those he wrought for
And the feet of those he fought for
Echo round his bones for evermore.

III.

Lead out the pageant : sad and slow,
As fits an universal woe,
Let the long long procession go,
And let the sorrowing crowd about it grow
And let the mournful martial music blow ;
The last great Englishman is low.

IV.

Mourn, for to us he seems the last,
Remembering all his greatness in the Past.
No more in soldier fashion will he greet
With lifted hand the gazer in the street.
O friends, our chief state-oracle is mute :
Mourn for the man of long-enduring blood,
The statesman-warrior, moderate, resolute,
Whole in himself, a common good.
Mourn for the man of amplest influence,
Yet clearest of ambitious crime,
Our greatest yet with least pretence,
Great in council and great in war,
Foremost captain of his time,
Rich in saving common-sense,
And, as the greatest only are,
In his simplicity sublime.
O good gray head which all men knew,
O voice from which their omens all men drew,
O iron nerve to true occasion true,
O fall'n at length that tower of strength
Which stood four-square to all the winds that blew.
Such was he whom we deplore,
The long self-sacrifice of life is o'er.
The great World-victor's victor will be seen no
    more.

V.　　·

All is over and done :
Render thanks to the Giver,
England, for thy son.
Let the bell be toll'd.
Render thanks to the Giver,
And render him to the mould.
Under the cross of gold
That shines over city and river,
There he shall rest for ever
Among the wise and the bold.
Let the bell be toll'd :
And a reverent people behold
The towering car, the sable steeds :
Bright let it be with his blazon'd deeds,
Dark in its funeral fold.
Let the bell be toll'd :
And a deeper knell in the heart be knoll'd ;
And the sound of the sorrowing anthem roll'd
Thro' the dome of the golden cross ;
And the volleying cannon thunder his loss ;
He knew their voices of old.
For many a time in many a clime
His captain's-ear has heard them boom,
Bellowing victory, bellowing doom :
When he with those deep voices wrought,
Guarding realms and kings from shame ;

With those deep voices our dead captain taught
The tyrant, and asserts his claim
In that dread sound to the great name,
Which he has worn so pure of blame,
In praise and in dispraise the same,
A man of well-attemper'd frame.
O civic muse, to such a name,
To such a name for ages long,
To such a name,
Preserve a broad approach of fame,
And ever-echoing avenues of song.

VI.

Who is he that cometh, like an honour'd guest,
With banner and with music, with soldier and with
    priest,
With a nation weeping, and breaking on my rest?
Mighty Seaman, this is he
Was great by land as thou by sea.
Thine island loves thee well, thou famous man,
The greatest sailor since our world began.
Now, to the roll of muffled drums,
To thee the greatest soldier comes ;
For this is he
Was great by land as thou by sea ;
His foes were thine ; he kept us free ;
O give him welcome, this is he

Worthy of our gorgeous rites,
And worthy to be laid by thee ;
For this is England's greatest son,
He that gain'd a hundred fights,
Nor ever lost an English gun ;
This is he that far away
Against the myriads of Assaye
Clash'd with his fiery few and won ;
And underneath another sun,
Warring on a later day,
Round affrighted Lisbon drew
The treble works, the vast designs
Of his labour'd rampart-lines,
Where he greatly stood at bay,
Whence he issued forth anew,
And ever great and greater grew,
Beating from the wasted vines
Back to France her banded swarms,
Back to France with countless blows,
Till o'er the hills her eagles flew
Beyond the Pyrenean pines,
Follow'd up in valley and glen
With blare of bugle, clamour of men,
Roll of cannon and clash of arms,
And England pouring on her foes.
Such a war had such a close.
Again their ravening eagle rose
In anger, wheel'd on Europe-shadowing wings,

And barking for the thrones of kings ;
Till one that sought but Duty's iron crown
On that loud sabbath shook the spoiler down ;
A day of onsets of despair !
Dash'd on every rocky square
Their surging charges foam'd themselves away ;
Last, the Prussian trumpet blew ;
Thro' the long-tormented air
Heaven flash'd a sudden jubilant ray,
And down we swept and charged and overthrew.
So great a soldier taught us there
What long-enduring hearts could do,
In that world-earthquake, Waterloo !
Mighty Seaman, tender and true,
And pure as he from taint of craven guile,
O saviour of the silver-coasted isle,
O shaker of the Baltic and the Nile,
If aught of things that here befall
Touch a spirit among things divine,
If love of country move thee there at all,
Be glad, because his bones are laid by thine !
And thro' the centuries let a people's voice
In full acclaim,
A people's voice,
The proof and echo of all human fame,
A people's voice, when they rejoice
At civic revel and pomp and game,
Attest their great commander's claim

With honour, honour, honour, honour to him,
Eternal honour to his name.

VII.

A people's voice ! we are a people yet.
Tho' all men else their nobler dreams forget,
Confused by brainless mobs and lawless Powers ;
Thank Him who isled us here, and roughly set
His Briton in blown seas and storming showers,
We have a voice, with which to pay the debt
Of boundless love and reverence and regret
To those great men who fought and kept it ours,
And keep it ours, O God, from brute control ;
O Statesmen, guard us, guard the eye, the soul
Of Europe, keep our noble England whole,
And save the one true seed of freedom sown
Betwixt a people and their ancient throne,
That sober freedom out of which there springs
Our loyal passion for our temperate kings ;
For, saving that, ye help to save mankind,
Till public wrong be crumbled into dust,
And drill the raw world for the march of mind,
Till crowds at length be sane and crowns be just.
But wink no more in slothful overtrust.
Remember him who led your hosts ;
He bad you guard the sacred coasts.
Your cannons moulder on the seaward wall ;
His voice is silent in your council-hall

For ever ; and whatever tempests lour
For ever silent ; even if they broke
In thunder, silent ; yet remember all
He spoke among you, and the Man who spoke ;
Who never sold the truth to serve the hour,
Nor palter'd with Eternal God for power ;
Who let the turbid streams of rumour flow
Thro' either babbling world of high and low ;
Whose life was work, whose language rife
With rugged maxims hewn from life ;
Who never spoke against a foe ;
Whose eighty winters freeze with one rebuke
All great self-seekers trampling on the right :
Truth-teller was our England's Alfred named ;
Truth-lover was our English Duke ;
Whatever record leap to light,
He never shall be shamed.

VIII.

Lo, the leader in these glorious wars
Now to glorious burial slowly borne,
Follow'd by the brave of other lands,
He, on whom from both her open hands
Lavish Honour shower'd all her stars,
And affluent Fortune emptied all her horn.
Yea, let all good things await
Him who cares not to be great,
But as he saves or serves the state.

Not once or twice in our rough island-story,
The path of duty was the way to glory :
He that walks it, only thirsting
For the right, and learns to deaden
Love of self, before his journey closes,
He shall find the stubborn thistle bursting
Into glossy purples, which outredden
All voluptuous garden-roses.
Not once or twice in our fair island-story,
The path of duty was the way to glory :
He that ever following her commands,
On with toil of heart and knees and hands,
Thro' the long gorge to the far light has won
His path upward and prevail'd,
Shall find the toppling crags of Duty scaled
Are close upon the shining table-lands
To which our God Himself is moon and sun.
Such was he : his work is done :
But while the races of mankind endure,
Let his great example stand
Colossal, seen of every land,
And keep the soldier firm, the statesman pure :
Till in all lands and thro' all human story
The path of duty be the way to glory :
And let the land whose hearths he saved from shame
For many and many an age proclaim
At civic revel and pomp and game,
And when the long-illumined cities flame,

Their ever-loyal iron leader's fame,
With honour, honour, honour, honour to him,
Eternal honour to his name.

IX.

Peace, his triumph will be sung
By some yet unmoulded tongue
Far on in summers that we shall not see:
Peace, it is a day of pain
For one about whose patriarchal knee
Late the little children clung:
O peace, it is a day of pain
For one upon whose hand and heart and brain
Once the weight and fate of Europe hung.
Ours the pain, be his the gain!
More than is of man's degree
Must be with us, watching here
At this our great solemnity.
Whom we see not we revere,
We revere, and we refrain
From talk of battles loud and vain,
And brawling memories all too free
For such a wise humility
As befits a solemn fane:
We revere, and while we hear
The tides of Music's golden sea
Setting toward eternity,
Uplifted high in heart and hope are we,

Until we doubt not that for one so true
There must be other nobler work to do
Than when he fought at Waterloo,
And Victor he must ever be.
For tho' the Giant Ages heave the hill
And break the shore, and evermore
Make and break, and work their will;
Tho' world on world in myriad myriads roll
Round us, each with different powers,
And other forms of life than ours,
What know we greater than the soul?
On God and Godlike men we build our trust.
Hush, the Dead March wails in the people's ears:
The dark crowd moves, and there are sobs and tears
The black earth yawns: the mortal disappears;
Ashes to ashes, dust to dust;
He is gone who seem'd so great.—
Gone; but nothing can bereave him
Of the force he made his own
Being here, and we believe him
Something far advanced in State,
And that he wears a truer crown
Than any wreath that man can weave him.
Speak no more of his renown,
Lay your earthly fancies down,
And in the vast cathedral leave him.
God accept him, Christ receive him.

TENNYSON.

I

XLIV.

THE LOSS OF THE BIRKENHEAD

1852.

(Supposed to be told by a Soldier who survived.)

RIGHT on our flank the crimson sun went down ;
The deep sea roll'd around in dark repose ;
When, like the wild shriek from some captured town,
    A cry of women rose.

The stout ship Birkenhead lay hard and fast,
Caught without hope upon a hidden rock ;
Her timbers thrill'd as nerves, when through them
    past
    The spirit of that shock.

And ever like base cowards, who leave their ranks
In danger's hour, before the rush of steel,
Drifted away disorderly the planks
    From underneath her keel.

So calm the air, so calm and still the flood,
That low down in its blue translucent glass
We saw the great fierce fish, that thirst for blood,
    Pass slowly, then re-pass.

They tarried, the waves tarried, for their prey !
The sea turn'd one clear smile !   Like things asleep

Those dark shapes in the azure silence lay,
    As quiet as the deep.

Then amidst oath, and prayer, and rush, and wreck,
Faint screams, faint questions waiting no reply,
Our Colonel gave the word, and on the deck
    Form'd us in line to die.

To die !—'twas hard, whilst the sleek ocean glow'd
Beneath a sky as fair as summer flowers :—
"All to the boats !" cried one :—he was, thank God,
    No officer of ours !

Our English hearts beat true :—we would not stir :
That base appeal we heard, but heeded not :
On land, on sea, we had our colours, sir,
    To keep without a spot !

They shall not say in England, that we fought
With shameful strength, unhonour'd life to seek ;
Into mean safety, mean deserters, brought
    By trampling down the weak.

So we made women with their children go,
The oars ply back again, and yet again :
Whilst, inch by inch, the drowning ship sank low,
    Still under steadfast men.

—What follows, why recall ?—The brave who died,
Died without flinching in the hungry surf.
They sleep as well, beneath that fatal tide,
    As others under turf.

They sleep as well ! and, roused from their wild grave,
Wearing their wounds like stars, shall rise again,
Joint-heirs with Christ, because they died to save
　　His weak ones, not in vain.

DOYLE.

XLV.

BATTLE OF THE ALMA.

THOUGH till now ungraced in story, scant although thy
　　waters be,
Alma, roll those waters proudly, proudly roll them to
　　the sea.

Yesterday unnamed, unhonour'd, but to wandering
　　Tartar known,
Now thou art a voice for ever to the world's four
　　quarters blown.

In two nations' annals graven thou art now a deathless
　　name,
And a star for ever shining in their firmament of fame.

Many a great and ancient river, crown'd with city,
　　tower, and shrine,
Little streamlet, knows no magic, boasts no potency
　　like thine ;

Cannot shed the light thou sheddest around many
a living head ;
Cannot lend the light thou lendest to the memory of
the dead.

Yea, nor all unsoothed their sorrow, who can, proudly
mourning, say,—
When the first strong burst of anguish shall have wept
itself away—

" He has past from us, the loved one, but he sleeps
with them that died
By the Alma, at the winning of that terrible hill-side."

Yes, and in the days far onward, when we all are calm
as those,
Who beneath thy vines and willows on their hero-beds
repose,

Thou, on England's banner blazon'd with the famous
fields of old,
Shalt, where other fields are winning, wave above the
brave and bold :

And our sons unborn shall nerve them for some great
deed to be done
By that twentieth of September, when the Alma's
heights were won.

O thou river ! dear for ever to the gallant, to the free
Alma, roll thy waters proudly, proudly roll them to the
sea.

TRENCH.

XLVI.

THE CHARGE OF THE LIGHT BRIGADE.

I.

HALF a league, half a league,
Half a league onward,
All in the valley of Death
Rode the six hundred.
" Forward, the Light Brigade !
Charge for the guns ! " he said :
Into the valley of Death
Rode the six hundred.

II.

" Forward, the Light Brigade !"
Was there a man dismay'd ?
Not tho' the soldier knew
Some one had blunder'd :
' Their's not to make reply,
Their's not to reason why,
Their's but to do and die :
Into the valley of Death
Rode the six hundred.

III.

Cannon to right of them,
Cannon to left of them,
Cannon in front of them
    Volley'd and thunder'd ;
Storm'd at with shot and shell,
Boldly they rode and well,
Into the jaws of Death,
Into the mouth of Hell
    Rode the six hundred.

IV.

Flash'd all their sabres bare,
Flash'd as they turn'd in air,
Sabring the gunners there,
Charging an army, while
    All the world wonder'd :
Plunged in the battery-smoke
Right thro' the line they broke ;
Cossack and Russian
Reel'd from the sabre-stroke
    Shatter'd and sunder'd.
Then they rode back, but not—
Not the six hundred.

V.

Cannon to right of them,
Cannon to left of them,
Cannon behind them
    Volley'd and thunder'd ;

Storm'd at with shot and shell,
While horse and hero fell,
They that had fought so well
Came thro' the jaws of Death
Back from the mouth of Hell,
All that was left of them,
    Left of six hundred.

VI.

When can their glory fade?
O the wild charge they made !
    All the world wonder'd.
Honour the charge they made !
Honour the Light Brigade,
    Noble six hundred !

TENNYSON.

XLVII.

FLORENCE NIGHTINGALE.

WHENE'ER a noble deed is wrought,
Whene'er is spoke a noble thought,
    Our hearts, in glad surprise,
    To higher levels rise.

The tidal wave of deeper souls
Into our inmost being rolls,
    And lifts us unawares
    Out of all meaner cares.

Honour to those whose words or deeds
Thus help us in our daily needs,
    And by their overflow
    Raise us from what is low !

Thus thought I, as by night I read
Of the great army of the dead,
    The trenches cold and damp
    The starved and frozen camp,—

The wounded from the battle-plain,
In dreary hospitals of pain,
    The cheerless corridors,
    The cold and stony floors.

Lo ! in that house of misery
A lady with a lamp I see
    Pass through the glimmering gloom,
    And flit from room to room.

And slow, as in a dream of bliss,
The speechless sufferer turns to kiss
    Her shadow, as it falls
    Upon the darkening walls.

As if a door in heaven should be
Open'd and then closed suddenly,
    The vision came and went,
    The light shone and was spent.

On England's annals, through the long
Hereafter of her speech and song,
    That light its rays shall cast
    From portals of the past :

A lady with a lamp shall stand
In the great history of the land,
    A noble type of good,
    Heroic womanhood.

LONGFELLOW.

XLVIII.

THE DEFENCE OF LUCKNOW.

I.

BANNER of England, not for a season, O banner of
    Britain, hast thou
Floated in conquering battle or flapt to the battle-cry !
Never with mightier glory than when we had rear'd
    thee on high
Flying at top of the roofs in the ghastly siege of
    Lucknow—
Shot thro' the staff or the halyard, but ever we raised
    thee anew,
And ever upon the topmost roof our banner of
    England blew.

II.

Frail were the works that defended the hold that we
   held with our lives—
Women and children among us, God help them, our
   children and wives !
Hold it we might—and for fifteen days or for twenty
   at most.
"Never surrender, I charge you, but every man die at
   his post ! "
Voice of the dead whom we loved, our Lawrence, the
   best of the brave :
Cold were his brows when we kiss'd him—we laid
   him that night in his grave.
" Every man die at his post ! " and there hail'd on our
   houses and halls
Death from their rifle-bullets, and death from their
   cannon-balls,
Death in our innermost chamber, and death at our
   slight barricade,
Death while we stood with the musket, and death
   while we stoopt to the spade,
Death to the dying, and wounds to the wounded, for
   often there fell
Striking the hospital wall, crashing thro' it, their shot
   and their shell,
Death—for their spies were among us, their marksmen
   were told of our best,
So that the brute bullet broke thro' the brain that
   could think for the rest ;

Bullets would sing by our foreheads, and bullets would
rain at our feet—
Fire from ten thousand at once of the rebels that
girdled us round—
Death at the glimpse of a finger from over the breadth
of a street,
Death from the heights of the mosque and the palace
and death in the ground !
Mine? yes, a mine ! Countermine ! down, down !
and creep thro' the hole !
Keep the revolver in hand ! you can hear him—the
murderous mole !
Quiet, ah ! quiet—wait till the point of the pick-axe
be thro' !
Click with the pick, coming nearer and nearer again
than before—
Now let it speak, and you fire, and the dark pioneer
is no more ;
And ever upon the topmost roof our banner of
England blew !

III.

Ay, but the foe sprung his mine many times, and it
chanced on a day
Soon as the blast of that underground thunderclap
echo'd away,
Dark thro' the smoke and the sulphur like so many
fiends in their hell—

Cannon-shot, musket-shot, volley on volley, and yell
    upon yell—
Fiercely on all the defences our myriad enemy fell.
What have they done? where is it? Out yonder.
    Guard the Redan !
Storm at the Water-gate ! storm at the Bailey-gate !
    storm, and it ran
Surging and swaying all round us, as ocean on every side
Plunges and heaves at a bank that is daily drown'd by
    the tide—
So many thousands that if they be bold enough, who
    shall escape?
Kill or be kill'd, live or die, they shall know we are
    soldiers and men !
Ready ! take aim at their leaders—their masses are
    gapp'd with our grape—
Backward they reel like the wave, like the wave
    flinging forward again,
Flying and foil'd at the last by the handful they could
    not subdue ;
And ever upon the topmost roof our banner of
    England blew.

IV.

Handful of men as we were, we were English in heart
    and in limb,
Strong with the strength of the race to command, to
    obey, to endure,

Each of us fought as if hope for the garrison hung but
    on him ;
Still—could we watch at all points ? we were every
    day fewer and fewer.
There was a whisper among us, but only a whisper
    that past :
" Children and wives—if the tigers leap into the fold
    unawares—
Every man die at his post—and the foe may outlive
    us at last—
Better to fall by the hands that they love, than to fall
    into theirs ! "
Roar upon roar in a moment two mines by the enemy
    sprung
Clove into perilous chasms our walls and our poor
    palisades.
Rifleman, true is your heart, but be sure that your
    hand be as true !
Sharp is the fire of assault, better aim'd are your flank
    fusillades—
Twice do we hurl them to earth from the ladders to
    which they had clung,
Twice from the ditch where they shelter we drive
    them with hand-grenades ;
And ever upon our topmost roof the banner of
    England blew.

V.

Then on another wild morning another wild earthquake
out-tore
Clean from our lines of defence ten or twelve good
paces or more.
Rifleman, high on the roof, hidden there from the
light of the sun—
One has leapt up on the breach, crying out : " Follow
me, follow me !"—
Mark him—he falls ! then another, and *him* too, and
down goes he.
Had they been bold enough then, who can tell but the
traitors had won ?
Boardings and rafters and doors—an embrasure ! make
way for the gun !
Now double-charge it with grape ! It is charged and
we fire, and they run.
Praise to our Indian brothers, and let the dark face
have his due !
Thanks to the kindly dark faces who fought with us,
faithful and few,
Fought with the bravest among us, and drove them,
and smote them, and slew,
That ever upon the topmost roof our banner in India blew,

VI.

Men will forget what we suffer and not what we do
We can fight,
But to be soldier all day and be sentinel all thro' the
night—

Ever the mine and assault, our sallies, their lying alarms.
Bugles and drums in the darkness, and shoutings and
    soundings to arms,
Ever the labour of fifty that had to be done by five,
Ever the marvel among us that one should be left alive,
Ever the day with its traitorous death from the loop-
    holes around,
Ever the night with its coffinless corpse to be laid in
    the ground,
Heat like the mouth of a hell, or a deluge of cataract
    skies,
Stench of old offal decaying, and infinite torment of flies,
Thoughts of the breezes of May blowing over an
    English field,
Cholera, scurvy, and fever, the wound that *would* not
    be heal'd,
Lopping away of the limb by the pitiful-pitiless knife,—
Torture and trouble in vain,—for it never could save
    us a life.
Valour of delicate women who tended the hospital bed,
Horror of women in travail among the dying and dead,
Grief for our perishing children, and never a moment
    for grief,
Toil and ineffable weariness, faltering hopes of relief,
Havelock baffled, or beaten, or butcher'd for all that
    we knew—
Then day and night, day and night, coming down on
    the still-shatter'd walls

Millions of musket-bullets, and thousands of cannon-
balls—
But ever upon the topmost roof our banner of
England blew.

VII.

Hark cannonade, fusillade! is it true what was told by
the scout,
Outram and Havelock breaking their way through the
fell mutineers?
Surely the pibroch of Europe is ringing again in our ears!
All on a sudden the garrison utter a jubilant shout,
Havelock's glorious Highlanders answer with conquer-
ing cheers,
Sick from the hospital echo them, women and children
come out,
Blessing the wholesome white faces of Havelock's good
fusileers,
Kissing the war-harden'd hand of the Highlander wet
with their tears!
Dance to the pibroch!—saved! we are saved!—is it
you? is it you?
Saved by the valour of Havelock, saved by the blessing
of Heaven!
"Hold it for fifteen days!" we have held it for eighty-
seven!
And ever aloft on the palace roof the old banner of
England blew.

TENNYSON.

K

XLIX.

ALBERT THE GOOD.

* * * * *

AND indeed He seems to me
Scarce other than my own ideal knight,
" Who reverenced his conscience as his king;
Whose glory was, redressing human wrong :
Who spake no slander, no, nor listen'd to it ;
Who loved one only and who clave to her—"
Her—over all whose realms to their last isle,
Commingled with the gloom of imminent war,
The shadow of His loss drew like eclipse,
Darkening the world.   We have lost him : he is gone :
We know him now : all narrow jealousies
Are silent; and we see him as he moved,
How modest, kindly, all-accomplish'd, wise,
With what sublime repression of himself,
And in what limits, and how tenderly ;
Not swaying to this faction or to that ;
Not making his high place the lawless perch
Of wing'd ambitions, nor a vantage-ground
For pleasure ; but thro' all this tract of years
Wearing the white flower of a blameless life,
Before a thousand peering littlenesses,
In that fierce light which beats upon a throne,

And blackens every blot : for where is he,
Who dares foreshadow for an only son
A lovelier life, a more unstain'd, than his ?
Or how should England dreaming of *his* sons
Hope more for these than some inheritance
Of such a life, a heart, a mind as thine,
Thou noble Father of her Kings to be,
Laborious for her people and her poor—
Voice in the rich dawn of an ampler day--
Far-sighted summoner of War and Waste
To fruitful strifes and rivalries of peace—
Sweet nature gilded by the gracious gleam
Of letters, dear to Science, dear to Art,
Dear to thy land and ours, a Prince indeed,
Beyond all titles, and a household name,
Hereafter thro' all times, Albert the Good.

  * * * * *

TENNYSON, *Idylls of the King: Dedication.*

NOTES.

I. "Constantinus, King of the Scots, after having
sworn allegiance to Athelstan, allied himself with the
Danes of Ireland under Anlaf, and invading England,
was defeated by Athelstan and his brother Edmund
with great slaughter at Brunanburh in the year 937."
Brunanburh was somewhere in Northumberland, but no
one knows exactly where.—*Dyflen* = Dublin.

II. In the reign of Athelred "the Unready" (979–1013)
there was a great invasion of the Danes, or, more truly,
Norwegians, in the eastern part of England. They
harried Ipswich, and then went into Essex, and sailed
up the river Panta, or Blackwater, to Maldon. But then
Brihtnoth, the Alderman of the East Saxons, came against
them, and there was a battle (A.D. 991), in which Brihtnoth,
after fighting very bravely, was killed. It was a great
pity there was so few men like him, who refused to pay
money to the invaders. Scarcely was he passed away,
when Danegelt began to be paid. This Brihtnoth was
very bountiful to the monks, and helped to found the
famous abbey of Ely, afterwards made a bishopric.
There he was buried, and there his wife Athelflaed offered
a piece of tapestry, on which she had worked the picture
of all her husband's great actions. This is the longest and

grandest of our old songs. Only the first half is given
here : of which also some lines at the beginning are lost,
and a few others omitted.—See Freeman, " Old English
History for Children," pp. 191–205.

III. " Though Harold had been chosen King by the
whole people of England, there were two men in the
world who fancied they knew better who ought to be King
in England than the English did themselves. These were
the King's brother Tostig and William Duke of the Normans. Tostig and Harold Hardrada King of Norway met
at the mouth of the Tyne, and Tostig submitted to him and
became his man, and they sailed together to the mouth
of the Humber, plundering as they went. And they
landed and went away to Stamfordbridge by the river of
Derwent. The news was brought to King Harold of
England, and he got together his host, and pressed on to
Stamfordbridge, and came upon the Northmen unawares.
And there was hard fighting for a long while, and many
men on both sides were killed, but in the end the English
had the victory, and King Harold of Norway and Earl
Tostig were killed."—Freeman, " Old English History for
Children," pp. 300–310.

IV. " The battle of Stamfordbridge was fought on the
25th of September, and four days later Duke William
landed in Sussex. . . . It was now Friday evening, the
13th of October, 1066, and all men in both armies knew
that the fight would be on the morrow. The English ate
and drank and were merry, and they sang the old songs
of their fathers. So on Saturday morning Duke William
arose early, and heard mass, and then marshalled his army
and made a speech to them. King Harold had also risen
early, and had put his men in order. . . . Very valiant
deeds were done by many men in both armies. They
had now been fighting ever since nine in the morning,

and twilight was coming on. But now the hour of our great King was come. Every foe who had come near him had felt the might of that terrible axe, but his axe could not guard him against the awful shower of arrows. One shaft, falling, pierced his right eye ; he clutched at it, and broke off the shaft ; his axe dropped from his hand, and he fell, all disabled by pain, in his own place as King between the two royal ensigns. . . . Then four knights rushed upon King Harold as he lay dying; they killed him with several wounds, and mangled his body. Such was the end of the last native King of the English. He fell by the most glorious of deaths, fighting for the land and the people which he had loved so well. . . . So many women came and took away the bodies of their husbands and sons and brothers. . . . And there was a lady called Edith, whom King Harold had loved in old times when he was Earl of the East Angles. So Edith went and looked for the body of King Harold among the heaps of slain English. And she knew him not by his face, which was all mangled so that no man could know him, but by a mark on his body." And some say that when she had found him, she too fell there beside him, and died ; and they brought their dead bodies together into the presence of Duke William.—Freeman, " Old English History for Children," pp. 317–339.

V. *Civil war and the Crusades :* two prominent features more or less apparent throughout the next three or four hundred years. The Crusades, a temporary and not unworthy outlet for the exercise of the heroic spirit, are here represented as a welcome relief from the unheroic miseries of civil war.

VI. "The future champion of English freedom was himself a foreigner, the son of a Simon de Montfort, whose name had become memorable for his ruthless crusade

against the Albigensian heretics in Southern Gaul. . . .
He had inherited the strict and severe piety of his father ;
he was assiduous in his attendance on religious services ;
his life was pure and singularly temperate ; he was noted
for his scant indulgence in meat, drink, or sleep. Socially
he was cheerful and pleasant in talk ; but his natural
temper was quick and fiery, his sense of honour keen, his
speech rapid and trenchant. But the one characteristic
which overmastered all was what men at that time called
his ' constancy,' the firm immoveable resolve which
trampled even death under foot in its loyalty to the right.
The motto which Edward the First chose as his device,
' Keep troth,' was far truer as the device of Earl Simon.
. . . While other men wavered and faltered and fell away,
the enthusiastic love of the people gathered itself round
the stern, grave soldier who ' stood like a pillar,' unshaken by promise or threat or fear of death, by the oath
he had sworn."— Green, " Short History of the English
People," pp. 148, 149.

The lines given are translated from a Latin poem of
the time in Creighton's " Life of Simon de Montfort."

The battle of Lewes was fought May 14, 1264.

VII. The battle of Cressy was fought on the 26th of
August, 1346. " The king (Edward the Third) ordered
his men-at-arms to dismount, and drew up his forces on
a low rise sloping gently to the south-east, with a wind-
mill on its summit, from which he could overlook the
whole field of battle. . . . At vespers the fight began. . . .
The Counts of Alençon and Flanders, at the head of the
French knighthood, fell hotly on the Prince's line. For
the instant his small force seemed lost, but Edward refused to send him aid. . . . ' Return to those that sent
you, Sir Thomas,' said the king, ' and bid them not send
to me again so long as my son lives ! Let the boy win
his spurs ; for I wish, if God so order it, that the day

may be his, and that the honour may be with him and them to whom I have given it in charge.'"—Green, "Short History of the English People," pp. 219, 220.

VIII. These lines are from the "Poem of the Black Prince" by the herald Chandos, who had attended him in all his wars, and was probably present at the scene which he depicts. They are quoted from a translation by the late Librarian of the Bodleian, in Stanley's "Memorials of Canterbury," where the last years of the great Prince are thus described : "A long and wasteful illness, which he contracted in the southern climate of Spain, broke down his constitution. For four years he lived in almost entire seclusion at Berkhampstead, in preparation for his approaching end. The last time he was seen in public was as the champion of popular rights against a profligate court, as fearless in the House of Parliament as he had been on the field of battle. This was in April, 1376. On the 8th of June, in his 46th year, the Black Prince breathed his last. Far and wide the mourning spread when the news was known. Even amongst his enemies . . . funeral services were celebrated. . . . But most striking was the mourning of the whole English nation. Seldom, if ever, has the death of one man so deeply struck the sympathy of the English people."

IX. The battle of Neville's Cross took place a few months after Cressy. A Scotch army burst into the North, was routed near Durham, and its king, David, taken prisoner, October, 1346. The ballad is reprinted in this volume by the kind permission of the publishers, Sampson Low, Marston, and Co., from "The Boys' Froissart," by Sidney Lanier. It contains a fine illustration of the following remarks of the historian :—"The whole social and political fabric of the Middle Ages rested upon a military base, and its base was suddenly withdrawn. The churl had struck down the noble ; the bondsman proved more than a match, in sheer hard fighting, for the knight. From the day of Cressy feudalism tottered slowly but surely to its grave."—Green, " Short History of the English People," p. 221.

X. " The song of Chevy Chase," wrote Addison, " is the favourite ballad of the common people of England ; and Ben Jonson used to say that he had rather have been the author of it than of all his works." The ballad, without being historical, may have had some foundation in fact. The law of the marches interdicted either nation from hunting on the borders of the other, without leave from the proprietors or their deputies. The long rivalry between the martial families of Percy and Douglas must have burst into many sharp feuds and little incursions not recorded in history ; and the old ballad of the " Hunting a' the Cheviat," which was the original title, may have sprung out of such a quarrel.—Percy, " Reliques of Ancient English Poetry." The spelling in this ballad is modernized, as far as possible, except where the change would interfere with the rhyme. *In the mauger of,* in spite of ; *shires three,* the shires of Holy Island, of Norham, and of Bamborough, all in Northumberland ; *bickarte,* skirmished ; *monynday,* Monday ; *mort,* the notes blown on the horn at the stag's death ; *on sides sheer,* on all sides ; *brittling,* cutting up ; *verament,* truly ; *meany,* company ; *glede,* red-hot coal ; *upon a party,* apart ; *basnets,* helmets ; *swapte,* exchanged blows, or dints ; *freckys,* men, fellows ; *dight,* promise ; *spendyd,* grasped ; *corsiare,* courser, steed ; *blane,* lingered ; *freake,* man ; *dre,* endure ; *hinde,* gentle ; *carpe of care,* complain through care ; *brook,* enjoy ; *Hombylldown,* fought September 14th, 1402, the English under Northumberland and Hotspur gaining a complete victory over the Scots ; *balys,* bales, ills ; *bete,* abate, remedy.

XI. John, Duke of Lancaster, surnamed of Gaunt, the now aged son of Edward the Third, and brother of the Black Prince, uplifts his dying voice against the degeneracy of his country, for which he had seen in his younger days so glorious a heritage laid up, it would seem, in vain. He died in 1399 ; the year in which his own son, Bolingbroke, Duke of Hereford, became King Henry the Fourth.

XII. Prince Henry of Monmouth, the son of Bolingbroke and grandson of Gaunt, is destined to restore the lustre of the earlier generation. Shakspere's ideal English hero ; exhibited in "the transition from boyhood to adult years, and from chartered freedom to the solemn responsibilities of a great ruler." In this passage " he stands before his father, able to maintain with truth that his nature is substantially sound and untainted, and capable of redeeming itself from all past, superficial dishonour."—Professor Dowden, " Shakspere : His Mind and Art," p. 212. *Percy, Hotspur:* see next note.

XIII. *The two Harrys:* Monmouth, the Prince of Wales, and Hotspur, the younger Percy, heir to the Earl of Northumberland. The king had offended the Percys, and Hotspur was on the march from the North to join the Welsh who were in rebellion. Harry, the Prince, was seventeen when in the company of his father he met the other Harry, a worthy antagonist, and his rival in glory of arms, and defeated and slew him at the battle of Shrewsbury, July, 1403.

XIV. These two speeches are addressed by the Prince and his Father, in the King's camp near Shrewsbury, to the envoy of Hotspur, his uncle, Thomas Percy, Earl of Worcester. The King sends the " offer of his grace," if Hotspur will lay down his arms.

XV. The reception of his envoy by the prince is reported to Hotspur in the rebel camp by Sir Richard Vernon, who accompanied the Earl of Worcester at the interview.

XVI., XVII. Professor Dowden thus sums up his criticism of the poet's ideal Englishman :—" Instead of constructing a strong but careful life for himself, life breathed through him, and blossomed into a glorious enthusiasm of existence. . . . The honour that Henry covets is not that which Hotspur is ambitious after . . . it is the achievement of great deeds, not the words of men which vibrate around such deeds. . . . Henry's freedom from egoism, his modesty, his integrity, his joyous humour, his practical piety, his habit of judging things by natural and not artificial standards ; all these are various developments of the central element of his character, his noble realization of fact." And he adds, " The same noble and disinterested loyalty to the truth of things renders it easy, natural, and indeed inevitable, that Henry should confirm in his office the Chief Justice who had formerly executed the law against himself."

XVIII.—XXI. Of the Agincourt campaign it must not be disguised that "no claim could have been more utterly baseless than the claim of the French crown by Henry the Fifth ; . . . and not only the claim, but the very nature of the war itself was wholly different from that of Edward the Third. Edward had been forced into the struggle against his will by the ceaseless attacks of France, and his claim of the crown was a mere afterthought to secure the alliance of Flanders. The war of Henry, on the other hand, though in form a mere renewal of the earlier struggle, was in fact a wanton aggression on the part of a nation tempted by the helplessness of its opponent, and still galled by the memory of former defeat."—Green, " Short History of the English People,"

p. 261. To come to the battle : " Henry had no choice between attack and unconditional surrender. His troops were starving, and the way to Calais lay across the French army. But the king's courage rose with the peril. A knight—it was said—in his train wished that the thousands of stout warriors lying idle that night in England had been standing in his ranks. Henry answered with a burst of scorn. ' I would not have a single man more,' he replied. ' If God gives us the victory, it will be plain that we owe it to His grace. If not, the fewer we are, the less loss for England.' Starving and sick as were the handful of men whom he led, they shared the spirit of their leader. As the chill rainy night passed away, his archers bared their arms and breasts to give fair play to ' the crooked stick and the grey goose wing,' but for which—as the rhyme ran—' England were but a fling,' and with a great shout sprang forward to the attack."
—*Ibid.*

XXII. Thirty-eight years after Agincourt, the English were struggling to retain a last remnant of their dominion in France. In 1453 a final effort for the southern territory so long held by us was made by the valiant and experienced soldier, John Talbot, Earl of Shrewsbury. He and his brave son, either of whom would have gladly died to save the other, were both slain ; Bordeaux was lost ; and, happily for England, the dominion of English kings in France came to an end.

XXIII. The doom hour of a tyrant. The Earl of Richmond, afterwards King Henry the Seventh, has appeared as the deliverer of his people from the odious government of Richard the Third, August 22, 1485.

XXIV. *Hugh Latimer,* sometime Bishop of Worcester ; *Nicholas Ridley,* Bishop of London ; and *Thomas Cranmer,*

Archbishop of Canterbury, the great leaders of the Reformation under Edward the Sixth, sealed their testimony
with their lives in the violent reaction under Queen Mary,
1555–56. "Latimer and Ridley were drawn from their
prisons at Oxford. 'Play the man, Master Ridley,' cried
the old preacher of the Reformation, as the flames shot up
around him ; 'we shall this day light such a candle, by
God's grace, in England, as I trust shall never be put out.'"
"One victim remained. . . . The courage which Cranmer
had shown since the accession of Mary gave way the
moment his final sentence was announced ;" and he
sought to purchase his pardon by recantation. "But
pardon was impossible ; and Cranmer's strangely mingled
nature found a power in its very weakness when he was
brought into the Church of St. Mary to repeat his recantation on the way to the stake. . . . 'Forasmuch,' he
concluded his address, 'forasmuch as my hand offended
in writing [such recantation] contrary to my heart, my
hand therefore shall be the first punished : for if I come
to the fire, it shall be the first burnt.' 'This was the hand
that wrote it,' he again exclaimed at the stake . . . and
holding it steadily in the flame, he 'never stirred nor
cried ' till life was gone."—Green, " Short History of the
English People," pp. 359, 360.

XXV. The purpose of the Spanish expedition was to
crush Protestantism in England, to establish the Inquisition, and so deprive the Netherlands, which had
revolted from Spain, of support from this country. The
Armada consisted of 136 ships, the English fleet only
numbering thirty-four. This, however, was speedily
augmented by some 160 volunteered merchant vessels.
The Londoners were asked for five thousand men and
fifteen ships. " Take ten thousand men," they said, " and
thirty ships," and they soon had them ready. " The
whole commonalty of England," writes Stowe, "became

of one heart and mind." The Queen, reviewing her troops at Tilbury fort, near London, declared that "she had the arm of a woman, but the heart of a king, and a king of England too, and thought foul scorn of any Spaniard who dared think of setting his foot on English soil." On the 19th of July the enemy was first sighted. On the 21st they met. "We pluck their feathers by little and little," wrote the English Admiral Howard, a few days later. On the 27th the last fight took place, when the great storm arose which completed their destruction. "God give us grace," Drake had written, "to depend upon Him, so shall we not doubt victory, for our cause is good." *Aurigny's isle*, Alderney ; *Edge-cumbe*, seat of Lord Mount Edgecumbe, in Plymouth Bay ; *Picard field*, Cressy (note on No. VII.) ; *Cæsar's eagle shield*, the standard of the "Holy Roman Empire ;" *Longleat* House, in Wiltshire, seat of the Marquis of Bath ; *Cranbourne* Chase, on the borders of Wilts and Dorset, seat of Lord Salisbury ; *Beaulieu*, in Hampshire, on the south-east border of the New Forest ; *Belvoir* castle, the Duke of Rutland's, in the north-east corner of Leicestershire ; *Gaunt's embattled pile*, Lancaster castle, built by John of Gaunt ; see note on No. XI. This poem is inserted by the kind permission of Messrs. Longmans and Co.

XXVI. According to Allen ("Battles of the British Navy," vol. i. p. 22), the English fleet consisted of seven ships, namely, the *Defiance, Revenge, Nonpareil, Bona-venture, Lion, Foresight*, and *Crane*. The Spaniards, it is said, lost nearly a thousand men before they subdued their brave enemy. For the original contemporary account see Arber's *English Reprints*: "The Last Fight of the Revenge, 1591." In Allen's list the *Nonpareil* appears to be an interloper.

XXVII. The father of *Oliver Cromwell* and the mother

of *John Hampden* were brother and sister ; so that Cromwell and Hampden were first cousins. In 1637–8, at the
ages of thirty-eight and forty-three, respectively, disgusted
at the proceedings of the court, and the recent decision of
the ship-money case in favour of the crown, they are
fabled to have engaged their passage to New England
in one of eight emigrant ships then lying in the Thames.
The vessel was, however, detained by a proclamation for-
bidding such embarkation unless under a licence from
Government. The relinquishment of the project is attri-
buted by the poet to Cromwell's change of purpose, forced
upon him by that " inward voice," which, like Socrates, he
acknowledged as his guide, and impressed by him with a
solemn and earnest eloquence upon his cousin.

XXVIII. Milton's picture of an English statesman. In
the Council of State appointed after the death of Charles
the First, in which John Milton was Latin Secretary, *Sir
Henry Vane* was entrusted with the administration of the
navy. Vane was a leader of the Independents, and
steadily opposed the force put upon the Parliament by the
army, the execution of the King, and the subsequent
usurpation of Cromwell. After the Restoration he was,
contrary to all justice, specially exempted from pardon,
and was beheaded in 1662, at the age of fifty.

XXIX. This sonnet was written in 1648, during the
siege of Colchester : an appeal from the lips of Milton
to a grander field for heroism than that of war. " It is,"
says Mr. Pattison, " a hortatory lyric, a trumpet-call to
his party in the moment of victory to remember the
duties which that victory imposed upon them." Mr.
Pattison adds, " Of Fairfax's eminent qualities the sonnet
only dwells on two—his personal valour, and his supe-
riority to sordid interests. Of his generalship, in which
he was second to Cromwell only, and of his love of arts

and learning, nothing is said, though the last was the passion of his life, for which at forty he renounced ambition."—" English Men of Letters : Milton," p. 89.

XXX., XXXI. *William Pitt*, created Earl of *Chatham*, died in 1778. His career as a Minister of State began in 1756. " He at once breathed his own lofty spirit into the country he served, as he communicated something of his own grandeur to the men who served him. ' No man,' said a soldier of the time, ' ever entered Mr. Pitt's closet who did not feel himself braver when he came out than when he went in.' In the midst of a society critical, polite, indifferent, . . . cool of heart and of head, sceptical of virtue and enthusiasm, sceptical above all of itself, Pitt stood absolutely alone. He was the first statesman since the Restoration who set the example of a purely public spirit. He loved England with an intense and personal love. He believed in her power, her glory, her public virtue, till England learnt to believe in herself. Her triumphs were his triumphs, her defeats his defeats. Her dangers lifted him high above all thought of self or party spirit. His glowing patriotism was the real spell by which he held England. He was the first English orator whose words were a power—a power, not over Parliament only, but over the nation at large. The few broken words we have of him stir the same thrill in our day which they stirred in the men of his own." Moreover, he had an " inborn knowledge of men." It was Pitt who " had discerned the genius and heroism which lay hidden beneath the awkward manner and the occasional gasconade of the young soldier of thirty-three (*James Wolfe*), whom he chose for the crowning exploit of the war " which was to " destroy the French rule in America." Let us turn to Wolfe, and to the eve of that memorable enterprise, the scaling of the Heights of Abraham, and the storming of Quebec. " Not a voice broke the silence of the night, save

the voice of Wolfe himself, as he quietly repeated the
stanzas of Gray's 'Elegy in a Country Churchyard,' re-
marking as he closed, ' I had rather be the author of that
poem than take Quebec.' But his nature was as brave
as it was tender : he was the first to leap on shore, and
to scale the narrow path where no two men could go
abreast. His men followed, pulling themselves to the
top by the help of bushes and the crags, and at daybreak
on the 12th of September (1759), the whole army stood in
orderly formation before Quebec. Wolfe headed a charge
which broke the lines of" the French, " but a ball pierced
his breast in the moment of victory. 'They run,' cried
an officer, who held the dying man in his arms, ' I protest
they run.' Wolfe rallied to ask who they were that ran,
and was told ' The French.' ' Then,' he murmured, ' I
die happy ! '"—Green, " Short History of the English
People," pp. 728-737. Cowper's pessimism was not
justified by the event ; though there was some ground for
the poet's manly impatience. When he wrote, in 1783, "the
wisdom of English statesmen seemed at its lowest ebb ; "
and " the force of public opinion was unable to check the
most shameless efforts of political faction." It was at the
close of that year that the younger Pitt became Prime
Minister.—*Our Hampdens and our Sidneys :* John Hampden, grandson of the great Hampden (No. XXVII.), and
Algernon Sidney engaged (1683) in a conspiracy to shut
out James, Duke of York, from the throne after the death
of Charles the Second. This is often incorrectly and un-
fairly confounded with the Rye House Plot, which was
one of assassination. Sidney, and Lord William Russell,
another of the party, were executed. John Hampden,
the elder, died from wounds received in the battle of
Chalgrove, 1643, praying God, with his last breath, to
save his country.

XXXII. In 1789 the French Revolution broke out, and
in 1793 France declared war against England. After

Nelson's victory of the Nile in 1800, an armed neutrality of the Northern Powers left England alone in her contest with France. To break up this coalition, in April, 1801, a British fleet under Nelson appeared before Copenhagen. Denmark was forced to withdraw from the Northern coalition, which was finally broken up by the death of the Czar.

XXXIII.-XXXVI. *Sonnets dedicated to Liberty*, 1802-3. In March, 1802, the Peace of Amiens was concluded. "But the Peace brought no rest to Buonaparte's ambition. It was soon plain that England would have to bear the brunt of a new contest, but of a contest wholly different in kind from that which the Peace had put an end to. . . . Once chosen Consul for life, Buonaparte felt himself secure at home, and turned restlessly to the work of outer aggression. . . . England was now the one country where freedom in any sense remained alive. . . . With the fall of England despotism would have been universal throughout Europe, and it was at England that Buonaparte resolved to strike the first blow in his career of conquest."—Green, " Short History of the English People," pp. 795, 796. " It is a very difficult thing for us . . . to conceive the united enthusiasm which stirred the heart of England in those days, when every moment the invasion of the great conqueror of Europe was possible. The fleets of England swept the seas ; on every hill the signal beacons blazed ; 420,000 men were in arms ; . . . every boy felt as if there were strength even in his puny arm to strike a blow in defence of the cause of his country. The moment was like that of the deep silence which precedes a thunderstorm ; men's breath was held, as if they were waiting in solemn and grand, but not in painful — rather in triumphant — expectation for the moment when the storm should break, and the French cry of ' Glory !' should be thundered back again by England's sublimer battle-cry of 'Duty !'"—F. W. Robert-

son, "Lectures and Addresses," pp. 253, 254.   "The 'men
of Kent' (No. XXXVI.) is a technical expression applied
to the inhabitants of that part of Kent which lies nearest
to France, who were never subdued in the Norman invasion, and who obtained glorious terms for themselves,
on capitulation, receiving the confirmation of their own
charters."—*Ibid.*, p. 255.   The allusion to this tradition
loses nothing of its poetic force by the discovery that it
is, after all, not history but mere legend.

XXXVII. *The Coptic sands :* the shores of Egypt at
the battle of the Nile ; *Elsinore :* at the battle of the
Baltic (see No. XXXII.) ; *Trafalgar :* see next note.

XXXVIII. *Nelson,* "the poet's type of the ideal hero.
Indeed, England and all the world as to this man were of
one accord ; and when in victory, on his ship *Victory* (Trafalgar, October 21st, 1805), Nelson passed away, the thrill
which shook mankind was of a nature such as perhaps
was never felt at any other death—so unanimous was the
feeling of friends and foes that earth had lost her crowning example of impassioned self-devotedness and of heroic
honour."—Myers, "English Men of Letters : Wordsworth," p. 80.   The same writer adds, "The hero himself
is only seen as completely heroic when his impetuous life
stands out for us from the solemn background of the
poet's calm.   And surely these two natures taken together make the perfect Englishman.   Nor is there any
portrait fitter than that of *The Happy Warrior* to go
forth to all lands as representing the English character at
its height."—*Ibid.* p. 81.

XXXIX. *Robert Blake,* born at Bridgewater, 1598, after
winning his first fame as a soldier, by his brilliant services
at sea under the Commonwealth, mainly against the
Dutch and Spaniards, added permanently to the respect
and honour paid to the English flag.   He died as he

was entering Plymouth Sound, August 17, 1657, and was buried in Westminster Abbey. No greater name, save only Nelson's, adorns the records of the British navy.

XL., XLI. *William Wilberforce,* son of a merchant at Hull, went into Parliament at twenty-one, as member for that borough, and at twenty-five sat for the county. Three years later, in 1787, he first brought the question of the Slave-trade before the House of Commons. On his deathbed, in 1833, he exclaimed, " Thank God that I should have lived to witness a day in which England is willing to give twenty millions sterling for the abolition of slavery."—*Thomas Clarkson* was the son of a clergy-man and grammar-school master at Wisbeach, Cambs. In 1786 he got a prize at Cambridge for a Latin essay on the question Whether it is lawful to make slaves of men against their will ? The subject so took hold of him, that he devoted himself thenceforth to the work of procuring the suppression of the Slave-trade. It took him twenty-one years to " climb the obstinate hill " of prejudice and self-interest, labouring with unabating effort outside the walls of Parliament, while Wilberforce fought the battle within. Nor, when "the palm was won," could their "zeal" submit to " find repose." The wages they looked for were "no quiet seats of the just," but " the wages of going on." In 1807 the Traffic in slaves sprawled in the dust ; they were free to turn their hands against the parent monster, Slavery itself. It was nearly thirty years more before she, too, received her deathblow on the 28th of August, 1833.

To this note shall be added the name of a kindred spirit, outcome of the same new-born enthusiasm of humanity, the name of *John Howard* (1726–1790), who gave his life "to the cause of the debtor, the felon and the murderer," and the reformation of prison discipline ; displaying (in the words of John Foster, " Essays," 1805), " an inconceivable severity of conviction, that he had

one thing to do, and that he who would do some great
thing in this short life must apply himself to the work with
such a concentration of his forces, as, to idle spectators
who live only to amuse themselves, looks like insanity."

XLII. *Thomas Arnold*, head-master of Rugby School
from 1828 until his death in 1842 : the founder of the
modern type of English public school education ; the
prophet of "moral thoughtfulness ; " the champion of
spiritual liberty, and national Christianity. His " Life,"
by Arthur Stanley, is an enduring record of the high-
water mark of English character in the first half of the
nineteenth century. The verses, from Matthew Arnold's
" Rugby Chapel, November, 1857," are inserted by the
kind permission of Messrs. Macmillan and Co.

XLIII. *Arthur Wellesley*, afterwards and for ever Duke
of Wellington and victor of Buonaparte at Waterloo, was
born 1769, died September 14, 1852. His public funeral
took place at St. Paul's Cathedral on the 18th of Novem-
ber. *Mighty Seaman* (see Nos. XXXII., XXXVIII.) ;
Assaye, in India, his first victory in the field, in the
Mahratta war, September 23, 1803 ; *another sun :* he took
the command in Portugal, 1808 ; *that loud sabbath :*
Waterloo was fought on Sunday, June 18, 1815 ; *the
Baltic and the Nile* (No. XXXII., note). Much of this
Ode breathes a like spirit with that of " The Happy
Warrior," to which it forms a noble *pendant*. And what
Mr. Myers says of that ("English Men of Letters :
Wordsworth," p. 84) is true also of this. " If a poet, by
strong concentration of thought, by striving in all things
along the upward way, can leave us in a few pages as it
were a summary of patriotism, a manual of national
honour, he has his place among his country's bene-
factors with a title as assured as any warrior or statesman,
and with no less direct a claim."

XLIV. (By the kind permission of the author.) The *Birkenhead* steamship, conveying troops to the Cape, was wrecked by striking on a sharp rock off Simon's Bay, South Africa, February 26, 1852 ; only 184, out of a total of 638, being saved by the boats. The heroism of the soldiers, in the calm sacrifice of their own lives to the safety of the women and children, reached a height seldom attainable on the battle-field.

XLV. In 1854 the Russian Emperor claimed dominion over the Christian subjects of Turkey. England and France intervened to defend the interests of the Turkish Government. In September the Allies landed in the Crimea, and, marching on Sebastopol, met the enemy strongly posted on the river Alma. Here they won a brilliant victory, crossing the river in the face of the foe, and driving him from his position on the heights on the other side. (This poem is inserted by the kind permission of the author.)

XLVI. Towards the end of October, the Russians crept out of Sebastopol, and attacked the rear of the Allies. Repulsed in a severe hand-to-hand combat by our gallant Highlanders, they still retained possession of their batteries ; when the extraordinary order was given to the Light Brigade, only six hundred strong, to charge an overwhelming host and capture the guns. The execution of that order has crowned with immortal glory the name of the Light Brigade.

XLVII. *Miss Nightingale*, christened after her birth-place, was born at Florence, in 1820, of an old Yorkshire family, her father's home being at Lea Hurst in Derbyshire. To a naturally high degree of compassion for physical suffering, she added with every year intensity, experience, and practical wisdom. The enthusiasm of humanity which burned within her, found by-and-by its due scope

for action in the crowded war-hospitals of the Crimea ;
in which, at the head of a band of English nurses, she
pursued her labour of love for two years from her arrival
to the close of the campaign.   Returned to England, she
applied her skill and energy to the organization of a
system for the training of others to serve in the like
sacred ministry.

XLVIII. Exactly a hundred years after the battle of
Plassey and the birth of our empire in the East, the Indian
mutiny broke out, in May, 1857.   The British residents
in Lucknow, the capital of Oude, were shut up in the
Government Residency from the latter part of June till
the 17th of November, when they were rescued by Sir
Colin Campbell.   For "eighty-seven" days of this time,
from the beginning of July, when Sir Henry Lawrence
was killed, until the arrival of Sir Henry Havelock and
Sir James Outram on the 25th of September, the little
garrison, unaided from without, maintained its painful
and heroic defence against an overwhelming host of
beleaguering sepoys.

XLIX. *Albert*, the husband of Queen Victoria, and
titularly known as "the Prince Consort," died on the 14th
of December, 1861 ; having long since won for himself
an enduring place in the reverence and affection of the
people, whom he had learnt to love as his countrymen,
and to whose highest welfare, directly and indirectly, he
devoted himself in the very spirit of princely heroism.

PRINTED BY WILLIAM CLOWES AND SONS, LIMITED, LONDON AND BECCLES.

www.ingramcontent.com/pod-product-compliance
Lightning Source LLC
Chambersburg PA
CBHW021107020726
47500CB00003B/648